# ROAD TALES

# ROAD TALES

## A Rambling of Motorcycle Stories

## Steve Reed

iUniverse, Inc.
New York   Bloomington

iUniverse books may be ordered through booksellers or by contacting:

iUniverse
1663 Liberty Drive
Bloomington, IN 47403
www.iuniverse.com
1-800-Authors (1-800-288-4677)

Because of the dynamic nature of the Internet, any Web addresses or links contained in this book may have changed since publication and may no longer be valid. The views expressed in this work are solely those of the author and do not necessarily reflect the views of the publisher, and the publisher hereby disclaims any responsibility for them.

978-1-4401-1121-1 (sc)
978-1-4401-1122-8 (ebook)

"Mooned", "An Annual Odyssey", "Wish List", "Non Riding Skills", "The Ultimate Tourer", "Riding With Murphy", and "Summer Rides and Aliens" reprinted with permission of *Motorcycle Tour and Cruiser* and *RoadBike* magazines.

Printed in the United States of America

iUniverse rev. date: 12/15/2008

For my wife, Angela, without whose unending support and unlimited understanding, this book could not have been written. And for my riding buddies, past and present, without whom, there would be no stories to tell. You know who you are and you have my gratitude and my friendship. And to the riders I have yet to meet. Life is a grand road and I look forward to meeting you on it someday.

# Contents

# THE QUEST FOR THE
# ULTIMATE CONEY DOG

Since time immemorial, man has yearned and searched for certain artifacts and landmarks. The Holy Grail, Noah's Ark, King Arthur's Sword, Excalibur, the Garden of Eden, Atlantis, the Ark of the Covenant, all of these stir the hidden adventurer in each of us. And while these treasures hold a certain fascination and mystery themselves, they pale in comparison to the ultimate quest… the search for the ultimate Coney Dog! This elusive jewel had escaped detection for far to many years. Until now.

Before undertaking any quest, the object of desire must be fully understood. The goal of this quest was not to be merely a hot dog in some stale bun, but a true gourmet's delight. A quality frankfurter resting snugly in a warm moist bun surrounded by mustard, ketchup, onions, relish, and various other delightful gastronomic accompaniments. And of course, it must be bathed in the finest coney sauce in the land. Rich meaty sauce worthy of a King's ransom. This entire ensemble would, if properly prepared, have the ability to make grown men weep with joy and cause women to swoon. This was to be no ordinary dog.

Two gallant knights, Paul "eleven is my limit" Crenshaw and Steve " hollow leg" Reed had agreed that this noble endeavor was truly worthy of quest status, so with full gas tanks and empty stomachs, we set out on this mission. Not for our own personal gain, but for hungry motorcyclists everywhere. Rather than follow the interstate's beaten path, we opted for back roads and adventure.

Heading south out of Trafalgar, Indiana (app. 30 miles south of Indianapolis), we chose to begin our odyssey on Salt Creek Rd. (or Sweetwater Tr. as it is also called). We both had traveled this road on numerous past occasions, but never on such a high and lofty mission. With the morning road unfolding before us under crystal clear skies, it was easy to settle back into the twists and turns of Saltwater Rd. Nothing to challenging, yet more than enough to keep your attention. For 18 miles, we danced with each curve and rise. Only one stop was called for on this stretch. Gatesville. For all the years we've been riding thru Gatesville, we've never been able to figure out if we were coming or going. Today was no different. The sign at the edge of town still withheld any clue.

Undaunted, we rode on. Brown County is one of the most scenic counties in central Indiana, and it's easy to see why. Tree covered hills rose up on either side of us. Quiet creeks ran alongside the road inviting us to stay awhile and splash beside their stony banks. Even the road seemed to say "slow down, fellows, life shouldn't be so rushed". With pavement as smooth and friendly as a puppy's kiss gliding beneath our wheels, neither of us could disagree.

At the end of Salt Creek Rd. is St. Rd. 46. East one mile, then south on St. Rd. 135 and the tempo picked up. Curves a bit tighter, rises a bit steeper. For the next 10 miles the dance became more of a tango than a waltz. No problem. We were up to it and with hunger making it's presence more than a little bit known (or was that growling merely Paul's bike backfiring?), we were about to face our greatest temptress on our journey.

Upon rounding a typical 15-mph curve, there she was. Lying there ahead of us. The Story Inn. A fine example of a Bed & Breakfast specializing in Hoosier hospitality. Oh yes, we knew she would be there, beckoning to us with her biscuits and gravy, her banana walnut hotcakes, her seasoned omelet, her fresh coffee and so many other temptations. Yes we would stop. Yes we would visit with Kristin, her manager. Yes, we would observe the renovations in progress and the barn being reconstructed for use as a Community House. Yes, the smells wafting from the kitchen were more than a little enticing. But with great physical and spiritual fortitude, we managed to mount our bikes once again and continue southward on our journey. Secretly, however, we both knew we would return another time.

Twenty one gorgeous, cornfield lined, wildflower drenched, log cabin viewed miles later, and we arrived at ST. Rd. 50. Not far now. Turning east, I thought I smelled coney sauce in the wind, but Paul was quick to point out that it was just freshly laid asphalt. Maybe I was hungrier than I thought.

Onward thru Brownstown, the county seat of Jackson County. Like all Indiana county seat towns, it has it's own quaint appeal. A courthouse sits in the center of town, surrounded by merchant shops with the town expanding outward from there. And yes, folks still sit on benches and wave at you as you ride by. Americana at it's finest.

Once Brownstown was behind us, we had only 8 miles to go and then there it was. It was our El Dorado, or as it is known locally Al's Heartbeat Café. A 50's theme diner complete with lunch counter. If there was a true Coney Dog to be found, it had to be here. Paul and I wasted no time parking the bikes and settling into a table. Glancing around the décor proved to be a feast for the eyes. Lots of 50's nostalgia items (complete with a full size fully restored "55 Chevy truck in the dinning room), plenty of posters and even a museum of restored classic cars behind the lunch counter. The entire dining area was decorated in a 50's motif right down to the '55 Chevy seat used as a waiting bench. You almost expected Richie, Potsie, Ralph, and the Fonz to step thru the door at any moment.

But back to our quest. Despite my protests, Paul ordered the classic 55 tenderloin and raved about it for the rest of the day. I went with the chili cheese dog and while I must admit it was very good, I would not qualify it as the ultimate coney dog. I feel no desire to weep nor did our waitress swoon. Oh well, the quest would continue another day. But wait! Could the fates have given us a second chance? It occurred to us that after riding 90 miles, perhaps we needed to look no further than our own back yard. Not 2 miles from my home is a "Dog and Suds Drive In". Carhops, window trays, and 10, count em', 10 varieties of dogs. A coney lovers idea of heaven. Thus inspired, we rode as though the devil himself was on our heels.

Interstate 65 North out of Seymour took us directly to exit 103 (Southport Rd.) and there in plain sight stood our redemption next to a new Harley Davidson Dealership. A coincidence? I don't think so. A quick survey of the menu placard and 2 coney dogs and a footlong coney dog were quickly on their way to our picnic table along with 2 frosty mugs of root beer. Superb. Although I still felt no urge to weep, I also felt no need to continue our quest that particular day. By the look of him, Paul wholeheartedly agreed.

Ah sweet mystery of life. The quest would always be there. Always patient, always waiting. Who knows? Perhaps the next quest should be the "Terrifically Tantalizing Tenderloin Tour". At least we know were to start

# ONE IS THE LONELIEST NUMBER

"I ride alone". That was his answer. I had asked a simple question and the answer I had received was direct and to the point. No pretense, no air of smugness. It also gave rise to another question.

"Why?"

That one caught him by surprise. "No particular reason. Just never hooked up with the right group of people I guess". We talked a bit more and after extending an invitation to ride together sometime, I went my separate way. However, the conversation we had kept running and rerunning through my head.

I ride alone. Sounds a bit strong. I ride alone. One can't help but conjure up images of a lone rider on a tired horse slowly making his way across a desolate, hot, arid, western landscape. Empty mile after empty mile. Nothing but the sound of his horses' hooves on the cracked, dry, earth to keep him company on his solitary journey. No future, no past. Just one lone rider going nowhere and never getting there.

Now don't misunderstand me. There are times I prefer the solitude of a quiet day ride. Sometimes one needs some "alone" time to sort out the frustrations and puzzles of day to day life. Riding by yourself is an excellent way to accomplish this. But to ride alone all the time? To do so seems like eating vanilla ice cream after every meal. Not bad the first few times, but what butter pecan, caramel swirl, chocolate marble, and dozens of others? Riding, like ice cream, comes in dozens of "flavors". 2-3 friends on a 200 mile jaunt, 4 buddies on a 3000 mile western adventure, 6-8 couples out for a 40 mile dinner ride, one good friend heading to Bike Week along side of you, 5 or 6 riders helping you straighten out 40-50 miles of tight, twisty curves, a crisp morning and a group of friends "doing it in the dirt" and grinning the whole time. Like I said, lots of "flavors".

Another thing. The lone rider on the prairie can have any number of adventures, but who shares them with him? Riding with a few friends can give any adventure [or misadventure] a whole new meaning. Shared experiences become lifelong memories. If you get caught in a sudden snowstorm alone, it becomes a survival contest. But get caught in that same snowstorm with a good friend and it becomes the basis for a great story told over and over. Being wet and cold in a driving rain is never any fun, but drying off in front of a roaring fire with a couple of rain soaked buddies makes the cold seem less frigid and the bone soaking wetness just a minor inconvenience. Stories are meant to be shared with a common audience and what better audience than the people who shared the last 600 miles together in 103 degree heat and are grinning at each other over iced tea at the end of the day. The spirit of a ride can be relived over a breakfast, a dinner, even a cup of coffee. But to do this best, the original event should be a shared one. The old axiom "2 heads are better than 1" is quite true, but, by the same token, "every story has 2 sides" is even more true.

One point here. If you choose to ride alone, that's fine. Have a great time. Just let people know where and when you're going. We really do care. Besides, you'll have some stories of your own to share and we'll want to hear them. However, riding with good companions gives you a bit more safety and security, should you need it. Something as simple as a flat tire or running out of gas can have two completely different scenarios depending on your choice of rides. Of course, if you choose to ride solo, there won't be any witnesses when you fill your bikes' gas tank with diesel fuel. Nor will there be any help. I would like to think that any rider would lend a hand if needed, but you just never know these days. It's a very special gift to ride with friends you can count on and I have never taken that gift lightly.

How you ride is your choice. All I can say is enjoy it in all its many forms, styles, or "flavors". Hey, anybody feel like some ice cream?

# THE GIFT

So it's Christmas Eve, he thought, who cares? Just another day as far as I'm concerned. He tried not to remember the excitement he felt, hiding his wife's presents through out the house, the look in his wife's eyes as she unwrapped box after box after box until she finally came to the diamond necklace buried in the last one, his daughters' face as she would gleefully tear open the packages. He tried not to remember the smell of Christmas dinner, the sounds of busy hands in the kitchen while it was being prepared, the sight of a child's handmade Christmas ornament hanging on the tree, the warm glow of contentment he felt watching his family on Christmas morning. He tried not to remember all of this and so much more, just as he tried not to remember the look on the officer's face when he had told him to follow him to the hospital. He tried not to remember the sight of his wife and daughter lying there hooked up to all those tubes and wires. The sounds of the monitors. The pulsing of the machines. The rain falling on 2 coffins as they were lowered into the ground. He tried not to remember the face of the drunk driver that crossed the yellow line, pleading in court for "just one more chance". Yeah, he had thought, like the chance my wife and daughter will never get. But it was pointless. He remembered it all and knew he would for the rest of his life.

Motorcycling had become his only pleasure in life. He owned 2 different styles of bikes, one for long touring rides, and one for the times he just wanted to get away. That bike had seen a lot of miles in the past 3 months and tonight would be no different. No radio to remind him of the holiday. No cassette tapes for company. No CB to listen to holiday greetings. Just him and the road. He had come to refer solitude to the company of others and tonight was a night for family and for children. No problem, he thought, At least traffic should be light. I feel most at home on the road anyway and this way I can avoid those consoling phone calls. He didn't decorate for the holidays anyway. No wreath. No lights. No cards. Not so much as a small tree. There just didn't seem to be any point in it. People thought he had become embittered, but that just wasn't the case. It was just to difficult, to hard to get into the spirit of things now. His reasons for "peace on earth and goodwill towards men" had been savagely taken from him and replaced with an empty hollow feeling. He truly believed Christmas would never be the same for him again.

Upon rolling the lighter of the two bikes out of his garage, he noticed the gas gauge was pointing hard to the left. Shouldn't put your horse away hungry, he mused. Looks like the gas station on the corner will be my first stop. Top off there and then be on my way.

As he fueled the bike, he couldn't help but notice a young woman fishing around in her purse and then in her car. She hadn't started pumping any gas yet and seemed upset. Maybe he should say something. No, don't get involved. Just go pay the attendant, get on the bike and go. Walking back to the bike, the woman caught his eye once more. However, this time she seemed to be softly crying. Oh well, I can at least show some Christmas spirit and see if I can help or something, he thought.

"Merry Christmas", he said. Even saying the words hurt more than he expected. "Are you having a problem?"

"Oh, no," she answered somewhat embarrassed "I need to get some gas and I'm just rounding up some change to pay for it." She appeared somewhat nervous and upset. He felt that from the look of her clothes and the car she was driving "rounding up some change" was a pretty common occurrence.

"Tell you what, how about I loan you a couple of bucks for gas being Christmas and all. I'm sure your family would rather see you get home before it gets to late." he said as he reached for a $10.00 bill.

"Oh no, I couldn't let you do that," she answered " my husband will be here in a few minutes and he's got some money. Besides, we still have to go Christmas shopping tonight for our son and daughter. They're at my parents for a couple of hours so we can get the shopping and wrapping done before they come home."

"I'll bet they're pretty excited, huh" he replied. That empty, hollow feeling was starting to grow. "Have you got a list made out already or are you just going to wing it?" At least he could be polite as he tried to make a graceful exit.

The woman burst into tears, "I don't know what to do," she sobbed. "We've managed to save a little money for the kids gifts and I know my folks are gong to give us money we can use to get tires for this old junker. My husband works down at the plant and weekends at a store, but there just never seems to be enough money to go around. I know it's hard when you're starting out. But does it have to be this hard? I mean, every time we start to get ahead, something happens. I got sick a few months back and we're still paying for that. I'm fine now, but it was touch and go for a few days. My husband never once left my side though, said he couldn't bear not to be there."

"I can understand that." the man quietly replied.

"Anyway," she continued, "times are tough and here it is Christmas. I think we've got the children pretty much covered but what about him? What do you give someone who sticks by you like that? I can't afford anything and he deserves so much. He won't tell me what he wants and I just don't know what to do. He means so much to me and I can't think of anyway to show him or tell him." The tears had slowed down now, "Listen to me go on like this. I'm sorry to have bothered you with my problems. I really don't want to sound like I'm complaining. I have 2 great kids and a wonderful husband. I'm a lucky girl and I know it."

"Sounds like it to me," he said. The pain was engulfing him now, but he smiled at her anyway. "Sounds like he's pretty lucky, too."

"I'm not so sure about that," she smiled back. "But as long as he thinks so, I suppose he is. Thanks for listening though. I really must have needed a good cry. I feel a lot better now."

"Some people say I have that effect on women," he said, trying to lighten the moment. Then it came to him. He knew what he had to do. Whether it made sense or not didn't matter. He only knew that he had to do it. "Does your husband know how to ride a motorcycle?"

"Well, yes he does. He had one when we got married, but sold it years ago," she stammered. "He said he'd always wanted to get another one, but it would have to wait until the kids were grown, or at least until our finances were a whole lot better."

"Not necessarily," the man answered. "Don't ask how or why or what the reason might be. See that red bike over by the cashier's office? That bike and I have traveled thousands of miles together lately. It has been more of a friend than a motorcycle. It has been there for me when I needed it most and has never let me down. It has taught me lessons I never thought I would learn and taken me places I could never had gotten to by myself. Now it can do something special for not just me, but you as well. My wife used to tell me that every gift is given twice. Once to the receiver and once to giver. I never understood that until now. When your husband gets here, hand him these keys and wish him a Merry Christmas. You'll find the title in the fairing pocket. I always carry it in case I want to trade bikes, but I never thought it would happen quite like this. I just filled the gas tank, so don't worry about "rounding up some change" he said. "Just consider it a Christmas miracle."

"But I can't . . ." The woman started to cry again, " You don't even know me. I can't possibly pay you. . ."

"You already have," he said gently, "If anything, I owe you."

But. . ."

"Wish your husband a Merry Christmas from someone who understands what a precious gift a family truly is and tell him to take care with the throttle. It's easy to over do it." Having said that, the man walked away into the fading light of the early evening.

The walk home only took 15 minutes, but they were the best 15 minutes he'd had in months. You were right, dear, when you tried to explain gifts to me, he thought as he walked. Now I finally understand what you were trying so hard to tell me. Once in the house, he still had the need to ride, but this time it was different. Not so much to escape from something, but rather drawn towards something. Well, I haven't ridden the big bike for awhile, he thought, and it would probably do us both some good. So, grabbing a jacket, a pair of gloves, and some riding glasses, he headed out to the bike. As he opened the trunk lid to retrieve his spare helmet, he noticed a card lying in the trunk compartment. Odd, he thought, I haven't gotten in here for months. Opening the card he read these words:

My life is complete because of you.

Thank you for being my husband.

Merry Christmas,

Your loving wife

When the man told me his story, he said that of all the properties, of all the houses, of all the vehicles, of all that he owns, that card is his most valuable possession. I would agree. He also asked me to share his story with you. I told him that I would consider it an honor to do so and so I have. Merry Christmas.

# MOONED AT 60 MPH

Awhile back, a group of us had gathered for a dinner ride. Nothing unusual about that. Dinners and riders go together like bacon and eggs or ham and cheese or french fries and brown gravy [yes , they really do go together]. We had chosen a particular destination that wasn't to far but, not to close, either. Someplace that would have good food and great coffee waiting for us when we arrived. After the usual tire kicking and route discussions, we were off.

As we pulled out onto the highway, I remember thinking what a great night for a ride. Temperature about 75 degrees, a light breeze out of the west, clear skies. Yeah, this was ideal riding weather. The group headed out and left the city traffic behind us in short order. Once we got past a couple of small towns, we could feel the countryside expand around us. The smells, the sights, the feel of being out on the bike, all of this was as intoxicating as 12 year old scotch without any of the unpleasant side effects. It was almost as if you could feel your soul relax, and then it happened.

Heading east on the highway, we noticed we were riding towards a rising moon. And what a moon it was! Poets would have called it a harvest moon and watching it rise over the cornfields, it was easy to see why. The brilliant white light illuminated the countryside with a soft, gentle glow. Craters were plainly visible on it's surface giving it the classic "man in the moon" look. You could almost feel him watching you, grinning his approval. "You really should come out and visit more often", he seemed to say, "I only do this a few times a month, you know.". Watching the moonlight reflecting off the farm ponds and streams as we rode by, you could almost feel the stress of the day fade away. Bikes lite up against the nights background, stars looking as though you could almost reach up and touch them, a brightly glowing full moon ahead of you, friends to share dinner and coffee with. Does it get any better than this, I asked myself? The shooting star off to my right gave me the obvious answer.

As we rode, you could sense a certain tranquility enfold you. Each rider was touched by it, each in their own, individual way. The destination was anticipated with both a sense of excitement and forlornging. We all were getting hungry, but no one wanted the ride to come to an end. The feeling of something wondrous and magical had woven it's way into the ride and all of us wanted to hold on to it for as long as possible.

Upon arriving, coffees and dinners were ordered and enjoyed. Conversations ran from bikes to rides to upcoming events and beyond. At the conclusion of dinner, our group split into various smaller groups, each group making it's way home via various routes. Everyone left with the knowledge that they had been part of something special, something different and unique. Maybe not very grand or elaborate, but very special none the less.

Do yourself a favor. Gather half a dozen or so friends and plan a "moonlight ride". Check the calendar to be sure that you're riding east into a rising moon on a late summer's night. Make the destination far enough to allow you to put the city behind you, yet close enough that you can kick back and have plenty of time for the return trip home. No tight schedules. Just you, some friends, the stars and moon above. Then you tell me - does it get any better than this?

# JUST DO IT

Ever notice how some rides seem to stand out more than others? The first time you got caught in the snow, that time in the rain after riding 100 miles in 95 degree heat, a hot summer's night ride with a full moon overhead and a good friend riding along side you, the ride you almost lost the bike but pulled out just in time. So many memories already, so many memories yet to be made. I was once told there are no bad bikes, some were just a little nicer than others. So it is with rides.

Some rides are grand elaborate affairs, lots of planning, making reservations, charting routes, calculating mileages and so on. Others can be as simple as a short jaunt to the store, for a few people, if they can't cover 200 to 300 miles during a ride, it's simply not worth it. Others find 40 -50 miles is all they need to feel satisfied. Isn't that what it's all about anyway? Satisfaction? You can't have a bad ride if you've been grinning at least 50 % of the time regardless of time or distance ridden.

The key to a good ride is to ride. You can't make memories sitting on the couch (at least these kinds of memories). It's so easy to think "Well, I can always ride tomorrow "or "I've only got an hour before dinner " or " There's no where to go ". Horse Hockey! Tomorrow never comes, dinner will taste better when you return, and there's always a road to ride somewhere. Some of us are finding to many excuses for odometers to remain idle. That is a loss that can easily be prevented. Like the commercial says - just do it. I know that my time riding is some of the best quality time I spend. Something about just being out, unencumbered by a car or truck, and going nowhere in particular puts things in perspective for me. Business decisions, job pressures, bills, day to day stress, all just seem to melt away with each passing mile. More then once my wife, in her infinite wisdom, has told me "Go ride somewhere, you'll feel better". She's right every time. Of course, I occasionally ride a little too far or a wee bit to long. This tends to prompt another variety of comments from her and again, she is usually right.

Ride whenever you get the chance. Be it a short open or a long haul. Make those memories and file them safely away. You'll be surprised how often you'll go thru them, even at the strangest places or times. Speaking of strange times, did I ever tell you about the time...

# INDEPENDENCE DAY

Traditionally, Independence Day is celebrated with cookouts, pool parties, family picnics, and of course, fireworks. All of these are great pastimes and are looked forward to by all of us. But take a moment and think about what this day really means to us. The " fireworks" that Francis Scott Key wrote about were certainly not Roman candles and anyone who had the courage to actually sign their name to the Declaration of Independence certainly had more to lose than a rained out barbecue. This independence which we so glibly celebrate was not an easy thing to come by. Men and women made life altering decisions over 200 years ago and continue to make them to this very day so that we can enjoy this precious gift called freedom. How many of us would literally give up family and home to fight for an idea. I don't mean sign a petition or write a letter or two, but leave your wife and children, your business, your fiends and go to a different land, endure poor living conditions, no pay, bad food, and actually take the life of another man before he takes yours. All this for the idea of a better life for your children and your children's children. I doubt there would be a lot of volunteers.

The old saying "freedom is never free " is painfully true. Ask any World War II Veteran. Ask any survivor of the USS Indianapolis. Then ask yourself "could I have made that sacrifice?"? Listen to a vet. describe Pearl Harbor or Pork Chop Hill or the Tet Offensive or any of the battles they made it thru and then listen to what they <u>don't</u> talk about. The ones who didn't make it. Imagine, if your can, standing on a dock and seeing everyone but your loved one come off the ship. Or getting a letter or telegram stating "It is my sad duty to inform you...". What's the price of freedom? It's a flag folded into a crisp triangle handed to a woman with tears on her face. It's a man learning to use a wheelchair for the rest of his life. That's the price of freedom. There are no refunds, no exchanges, no returns. Freedom has and shall always demand a high price.

Not a very light hearted article is it? Well there's nothing light hearted about freedom or independence. It's serious business. It's about as real as it gets. But it does have it's up side. Motorcycling is based on freedom. Freedom to choose what to ride, where to ride, when to ride, who to ride with, even why to ride. Freedom is what motorcycling is all about. Free to get away from the day to day grind, free to enjoy the road and all the wonders it has to offer. Free to challenge the elements or free not to. Free to gather with friends and agree or disagree on any topic. Free to cross borders without papers or checkpoints. Free to ride for an hour, a day, a week, a month. Free to customize your bike to your individual wants and desires.

And free to stop by a cemetery or graveyard and wander thru it looking for a headstone of a soldier or sailor. Keep in mid that their efforts played an important role in everything you enjoy today. Offering him or her a quite "thank you" would not be remiss. And if you hear "God Bless the USA " on the radio afterwards, don't feel embarrassed by that tear on your cheek or lump in your throat. I promise you'll be in good company.

# Letter To A Grandson

Dear Grandson,

Today you are eighteen. Congratulations. I bet you thought you'd never make it. I always knew you would, but I wasn't so sure if I would be around to have a piece of your birthday cake with you. So a while back, I wrote this to you just in case. Take this letter, go somewhere quiet, and read it aloud. I've always believed words should be heard as well as read.

Today you told me you wanted to "ride motorsickle". I told you no, we couldn't today. There was to much snow on the ground and your grandmother wouldn't let us. You said "I ride with you someday?" I said yes, someday you would. You grinned, walked away, and started to play with the dog. Your parents came and picked you up a little later and nothing more was said about "motorsickles". I know that a 3 year olds' attention span wanders constantly, but something about your question has stuck with me and I wanted to tell you something. Hopefully, you'll understand.

I don't know if the fates will allow us to ride together in the future or not. It'll be another 13 years before you can even get your drivers' license and probably another year or so before you get your motorcycle endorsement. I hope to be a part of your day to day life then, but no one really knows. There are some things I want to leave you, just in case I'm not around to give them to you personally. I feel they are important and you should not take any of them for granted. If you do, you will surely lose them. Sorry, money isn't one of them. That's something that is fleeting at best and should be earned by you, not handed to you. These items can't be purchased or traded or commercialized. Like I said, these are important.

Roads. Both good and bad. The feel of good pavement on a long ride. The hum of your tires on it. The serenity of going somewhere. The trip itself matters as much as the destination, perhaps more. Keep that in mind. Every road leads somewhere. With the right frame of mind, all can lead to adventure. Roads so bad, you'll swear never to ride again if God will just let you get off it. Roads with twists, turns, loops, hairpins, grades, gravel, mud, sand, snow. Wet roads and dry roads. Roads that take you away and roads that bring you home.

True friends. Not your run of the mill "you've got a new bike, so you can ride with us" friends, but the "Here take my bike, you gotta get home. I can grab a motel for the night." type of friends. Solitary riding is a wonderful thing and has it's own rewards, but most memories are of shared experiences. Remember, to have true friends, you have to be one. Be honest with them and show patience and tolerance. No one's perfect, including you. Don't ask more of them than you're willing to give. A true friendship is like a fine wine. It requires a special process that is not known by everyone. Time must be spent aging and seasoning it. You cannot rush or hurry it. If you try to, you'll spoil the end result. But, if you start with the right ingredients, such as honor, loyalty, humor, compassion, trust, and faith, you'll find that the results are worth the wait. Most people never have more than three or four true friends in a lifetime. If you can honestly say you do, you're a lucky man.

Sunrises and sunsets. Make the effort to watch at least one sunrise and one sunset every month, preferably while on your bike. Riding at these times has a magic all it's own that cannot be described. To watch a new day come to life and to be part of it is a privilege and should be treated as such. Sunset is a sign of that days passing and a glorious reminder that no day should be wasted. Pay attention to these things. Life is a fantastic journey and sunrises and sunsets are the milemarkers.

Fear. I mean the kind you can taste. Fear is important. It will keep you upright if you pay attention to it and drop you like a rock if you don't. Fear can be, and should be, controlled, but never ignored. It will help you learn your limits, but don't let it stop you from expanding them. Don't ride beyond your own limits. I knew a man who lost both legs simply because he didn't listen to his fear. "If Joe can ride that fast thru those curves, then I can." Stupid, pure and simple. Never mind what other people do or say. Believe in yourself. I do.

The feel of a good bike. It doesn't have to be a brand new, shiny, expensive, import or some classic piece of American iron. It does have to be yours. No payments to the bank. No high maintenance bills. No fancy frills. Just a good solid bike. Something you can ride 10 miles or 10,000 miles at a moments notice. A bike you bought with money you earned. A bike with only your name on the title. The right bike is a true joy to own, the wrong one is pure misery. Once you've got THE bike, be prepared to give a small piece of your soul to it. I did and have never regretted it for a moment. Hopefully, you'll understand the unspoken bond between the two of you. Your bike can make you smile when you're sad, laugh when you want to cry, and make you feel like a king when you're a pauper. It will humble you when you 're cocky and make you look like a better rider the you are. It can and will change your life, if you let it.

The love of a good woman. You'll need this one most of all. Not only in all aspects of life, but especially with regards to motorcycling. She'll need to understand your need to ride in bad weather, your desire to see distant places, the times you need to ride alone, your constant obsession for your bike, the trips with your buddies, and dozens of other things. Maybe she'll ride, maybe she won't. Regardless, she should never feel threatened by your riding. Instead, strive to make her part of it. Involve her in more than just the bike cleaning rituals. If you're out on a trip, call her so she can hear your voice. See that she knows you'll return from each and every ride. Take the time to let her know that she's special and that the best part of any ride is coming home to her. If you need a hand here, see your grandmother. I got lucky when I found her and tried to let her know it on a regular basis.

The rest of the things I leave you were left to me by my grandfather. Clouds, coffee in a thermos, rain, motorcycles, autumn colors, the smell of fresh cut grass, the sound of thunder, the feel of fresh snow underfoot, the look of wonder on a child's' face at Christmas, the amazement and fear you feel the first time you hold your newborn child, and so much more. Take good care of these treasures and when the time comes, pass them on to your grandson. And one more thing. Sometime when you're out riding at night, glance up and look at the canopy of stars above you. If you look hard enough, you might see me wink at you. Even if you're not sure, wink back. I'll be watching.

Love,

Grandpa

# ANOTHER RIDE

OK, you've done your chores, the bike is gassed, and your buddies are on their way over. There's a ride to be taken, but where to go? All of you have been on the same roads and are perhaps looking for something a bit different this time. Well, maybe I can be of some assistance. Pack a lunch, some cold drinks, and follow me.

We'll start by heading south on I-65 out of Indianapolis. I know, I know. You hate interstates. Sorry, but we need to make some time on the first leg of this ride. There'll be plenty of curves and scenery ahead. I promise. Once we get just north of Louisville, we're going to head west on I-265 and pick up I-64 West a few miles out. OK, we're done with the interstate once we arrive at the 114 exit. At this point, it might be prudent to gas up. Back on the road again, we'll continue south and meet up with ST. RD. 62 in Lanesville. Turn west here and "let the good times roll". We have about 120 miles of some of the best roads Indiana has to offer ahead of us and all afternoon to enjoy them. As we roll past the Overlook Restaurant on our left, make a mental note to come back here next October. The scenery is incredible here at that time of year. Continuing on, we'll do about 45 miles until we need to be looking for the next highway sign and that will be for ST. RD. 162 [of course, pay attention to the speed limit and curve signs during this part of ride or you'll be sorry].

At 162, we're going to turn south and go thru Santa Claus, In. [Steve Kirkendoll's real hometown?]. A bit further and we come to ST. RD. 70. East on 70 and in a few miles, we'll stop at a roadside park at the junction of 70 and 66. That lunch you packed should taste pretty good about now. A cold drink [or some coffee if you packed a thermos instead] would probably be a welcome site as well. Let's take some time here. A good stretch and a brief walk are certainly in order. Maybe a picture or two. OK, break's over. Time to saddle up.

East on 66 will take us along the Ohio River for quite a bit. Great scenery, but keep an eye on the road. You don't want to become a part of it. At Tell City, we'll gas up again. It's the best opportunity [if not the last chance] before P---- never mind. Just take my word for it. Following 66 will take us thru some of the southern most tip of the Hoosier National Forest. Friend, it doesn't get much better than this. ST. RD. 66 will eventually join with ST. RD. 37, at which point we'll head north on 37. This route will keep us within the boundaries of the national forest a bit longer. Paoli is up ahead and once thru it, the countryside starts to lose it's appeal. Oh well, it's been and still is a great ride.

As we head north on 37, I think a surprise is in order! In Bedford, the junction of 450 and 37 has the usual fast food establishments. However, if you look behind the McDonald's, you'll see our objective. Ritter's Frozen Custard! We deserve a reward after subjecting ourselves to the rigors and stress of traveling such gorgeous roads, don't we? Something about "to the victors belong the spoils" I think. Sure you can have a double scoop.

Once bikes and bellies have been filled, it's time to saddle up one last time. ST. RD. 37 rides like an interstate from here to Indianapolis, but that's OK. It's been a full day and "home" has a pleasing sound to it. The ride may be coming to an end, but the memories have just begun.

Thanks for having me along. Maybe we can do it again soon. Real soon.

# ONE VOICE

Have you ever wondered if you ever made a difference? I mean a real difference, not some little change in your day to day routine. Something that would or could change another persons' life? Maybe something as small as changing a tire on a rainy night for a total stranger stranded in the middle of nowhere or something as grand as donating a life saving organ to a child, waiting on the worst list imaginable. Some differences are readily apparent, while others may take years to be realized. Allow me to elaborate.

How many times have you said "have a good day"? Did you really mean it, or were you just being "socially polite"? Hopefully you were sincere in your salutation, as most people normally bear no ill will towards their fellow man. One day, however, upon uttering these words to a bank teller at the conclusion of our transaction I was startled by the reply. "Sir", she said, "Those are the kindest words I've heard all day. With all the problems and troubles I've had today, I didn't think there was much of a chance of salvaging the day. But I must admit, your thoughtfulness has made me reconsider. Thank you". A simple phrase, genuinely offered, had a completely unexpected and positive effect on someone's day.

Once during a ride, I made the usual gas, food, and rest stop. No big deal. Nothing out of the ordinary. Until a car pulled up to the pump next to me. A lady, possibly in her late 60's or early 70's, got out of the car so she could use the self serve pump. The difficulty she experienced simply operating the gas pump frustrated and confused her to the point that I walked over and offered my services. She smiled a little awkwardly and said if it wasn't to much trouble, she could use the help. It seemed that her husband had recently passed away and he had always taken care of the "mechanical things". We talked about him a bit and I learned that he had ridden a motorcycle for years. She had ridden with him an occasion and had enjoyed it, but thought that part of her life had died with him. I told her that was not necessarily so and if she would like to, I would be honored to give her a ride to anyplace she wished to go. She looked at me in disbelief for the longest time and slowly a smile crept across her face. "Do you really think I could?". She asked as if afraid to think it might be possible. "If you would like to, than I see no reason not to" I answered. With that, she went into the station and paid the attendant. "He said it would be all right to park my car over there until we get back. My daughter lives about 5 miles from here. Would it be to much to ask for a ride to her house? I'd be glad to pay for the gas." Now she was grinning from ear to ear. "I can't think of any place I'd rather go", I grinned back. The 5 miles went quickly and she told me to honk the horn when we arrived. "I want the family to see Mother's not as old as they might think." she laughed. Sure enough, when the family came running out to see what the commotion was all about, none of them were prepared for the sight of Granny on the back of a "motorsickle". Pictures were taken, questions asked, and more rides given. Upon my departure, I knew that those children would be bragging about the day Granny rode that "big ol' motorsickle". More importantly, I knew that those 5 miles would be the finest 5 miles I would ever ride.

A boy of young years doesn't truly comprehend the complexities and mysteries of life. But he does know how to wish, how to dream, how to hope. That black Bridgestone 125 was the biggest, baddest, motorcycle he had ever seen and he was standing right beside it. He didn't dare touch it and knew better than to ask how fast it would go. Grownups didn't like foolish questions, you know. None the less, he couldn't help but be drawn to that machine. Something about it kept beckoning him back time and time again. It was as though he was a fish on a line and the bike kept reeling him in. Even when he would lay in bed at night, he could feel it's pull on his soul. There was something mystical about that motorcycle and he was powerless against its' spell. The thought of actually owning something that grand, that powerful, that beautiful was more than he dared to imagine. Maybe when he was grown up and rich and famous he would buy that bike and it would take him on hundreds of adventures. Yeah. That's exactly what he would do. He'd show everybody what a person could do if they had a bike like that! So the next day, he went to see the bike again. But this time he had a purpose. However, as he approached the bike, his resolve started to crumble. It was so big! The speedometer went all the way to 80 mph! How could a person drive something so big so fast! It just didn't seem possible. His dreams of excitement and adventure started to fade when he heard a voice say "Want to sit on her?". He whirled around to see a man smiling down at him. "Are you serious? You'd let a little kid like me sit on this motorcycle?" the boy asked excitedly. "You won't be a little kid forever." came the answer. "Who knows? Maybe you'll grow up to be a motorcycle rider. You gotta start somewhere." Having said this, the man lifted the boy up and placed him on the seat of the motorcycle. Sitting there, the boy noticed the gasoline price on the sign was 24.9 cents a gallon. And he had not one, but TWO quarters in his pocket! All the excitement and adventure came rushing back, pouring over the boy like rainwater pouring out of a downspout in a thunderstorm. That one voice had made a difference. It opened a whole new world when it placed that small boy on the seat of that shiny black motorcycle.

To this day, it's still my favorite seat.

# GOING THE DISTANCE

Over the last few years, I have noticed a trend in various riders to see how many miles they can rack up on the odometer in a given length of time. How far they can go in a in a day, a week, a month, a year. Every trip is measured by distance covered, not desires fulfilled. Quantity not quality. I must admit that I too have fallen prey to "the mileage bug". Once bitten, it is difficult to resist. The challenge of doing 1000 miles in a day can be most intoxicating. The planning, the preparation, the stamina, the thrill of accomplishment. The Four Corners run, the Iron Butt Rally, and other distance rides have their own alluring appeals and certainly entice and ensnare more than a few determined riders. To these individuals, I tip my hat [or helmet] and wish them Godspeed and a safe journey.

As I notice my own personal "odometer" turning a bit faster than I might like, I find that miles ridden does not necessarily equate to enjoyable time in the saddle. Sure, I've had some long days that covered hundreds of miles and cherish those memories [bragging rights are rarely earned sitting at home in front of the TV]. But I am quickly learning that any ride is a good ride. Some are just a little better than others and that the difference is not always determined by miles covered. The quality of a ride depends much more on the attitude rather than the destination of the ride. I offer the following examples as proof.

Take a state map, spread it out, close your eyes, and point to a town. OK. There's your destination. Now next Saturday, ride there. But do so by using state or county roads only. No interstates. Once you've arrived, find the local diner [no national chains], go in, tell the waitress you'll have the special, sit back, and enjoy the surroundings. That older couple in the booth, wonder how long they've been coming here? Those two guys at the counter. Bet they're on a lunch break from the local store up the street. Notice how everyone glances at your bike as they're leaving? I'd wager that they wish they were on it riding somewhere, anywhere. Be sure to leave a tip when you leave. After all, Yankee pot roast wasn't the only flavor you enjoyed at lunch.

Another day, another ride. Pack a thermos and hit the interstate. About half an hour before sunset, pull into a rest area. Go over to a table, pour yourself a coffee, and watch the sun go down. Pay attention to the colors that God is using to paint the sky this evening. See how bright and vibrant they begin and how they slowly darken until even the last hint of red, blue, and gold fades away. Pour yourself another coffee. You're not leaving just yet. That first star you saw 15 minutes ago is quickly being joined by others, a few at a time. With any luck, the moon has risen by now. As the evening deepens, you start to notice the sounds of the night have begun. Crickets, frogs, even the howl of a distant coyote all join in the song. With the night enveloping you in it's own brand of magic, you walk back to your bike and fire it up. If you felt a twinge of an apology for disturbing the serenity of the moment, good for you. I've felt that same twinge.

A long, winding, road beckons you. This time, however, you ride it at 10 mph below the posted speed limit [traffic permitting, of course]. No pushing thru the turns, no hammering the straight-aways, no calculating apexes. Just a leisurely ride on an old friend. You've ridden this road a dozen times, but never quite like this. No hurry, no hot throttling, no tight leaning. Sure you could crank it up, but why this time? There will be plenty of other rides for that. Sit back and enjoy the ride for it's own sake. Find a good place to stop for a moment. Dismount, and thank the road for past pleasures and future challenges. Some believe that all things are joined, linked to one another by some unknown force in the universe. Maybe they're right, maybe not. In any case, that moment of gratitude will do more for your soul than you may realize at the moment. Appreciation works both ways.

Grab 6 or 7 friends and take off for nowhere in particular. After about 10 minutes, have the leader fall back to the last position. In another 10 minutes, that leader falls to the rear as well. Continue this procedure until the original leader is back at the point position. During the ride, all leaders should be encouraged to get the group as lost as possible, since it would be someone else's responsibility to get the group back on track. The larger the group, the more lost you can get. After a couple of these rides, you learn to have an eye for detail, believe me. One thing to remember, don't take this ride to seriously. Enjoy the companionship and tuck those memories in a safe place. You'll want to pull them out some cold winter night.

Show a new rider a favorite ride of yours. Teach them the best way to take that curve, how to handle that uphill stop, where to have lunch, what to watch out for along that wooded stretch. Remember the awe you felt in your early riding days, the sense of accomplishment you felt when you knew you "got it right". New riders are often intimidated by things you now take for granted. Put some of their fears and apprehensions to rest and do it with grace and respect. Encourage rather than criticize. Share mistakes you've made with them and let them make their own. Be supportive. Take the time to talk with them, not to them. Enjoy their enthusiasm as you would enjoy a cool breeze on a hot summer's night. Pass your experiences and skills on to them, openly and willingly. In the worst case scenario, you'll possibly bore someone for a short time. However, odds are that you'll help open a new and exciting world of adventures and limitless possibilities to someone who's just starting to take their first tentative steps. If you think back, I'm sure there was someone who opened a door for you. It's never to late to return that kind of favor.

Distance can be miles, kilometers, yards, even inches. Or, it can be days, memories, attitudes, or feelings. It's up to you to decide. Just go the distance.

# THE BEST OF BOTH WORLDS

Recently I had the good fortune to enjoy two different and unique styles of riding during my travels. One was the Lone Rider on the horizon and the other while in the company of good friends. Sometimes you can have your cake and eat it, too. Here's how.

My journey began as a promise to a friend to accompany him to Minnesota for a family reunion. I had never been to Minnesota and it sounded like an adventure. OK, count me in. We headed out and quickly fell into the rhythm of the road. After 2 days, we arrived at our destination. Check into a motel, family introductions, dinner, a good night's sleep and the following morning, I struck out for my next destination, 900 miles away, alone.

At first, the ride felt no different than any other ride. But as I got farther into it and deeper into unknown territory, small worries started to creep into my thoughts. What if I get a flat tire, what if I have an accident, what if I got lost, what if ... so many what ifs. After a short conversation with myself, I started to think more along the lines of what if I have a great time, what if I find the perfect breakfast restaurant, what if the sunset is incredible tonight? I started to like these "What ifs ".

As I rode on, I deliberately left the CB and radio turned off. The next 2 days were something I didn't want "commercialized". Without these distractions, I could truly become part of the ride, not just a rider. My thoughts rambled freely from Plains' Indians to homesteaders to winter storms to rest stops with good coffee to cloud formations and beyond. I found myself enjoying, even relishing, my solitude. I stopped when I chose, traveled roads I chose, ate where I chose. No conflicts, no pretense. Even more important I found that I trusted myself. I knew I could do this. Even enjoy it. Fear and apprehension had given way to confidence and exhilaration.

So the next 2 days went. Me listening to the sounds of drums and chanting blowing across the prairie from over a century ago and hoping dinner would taste as good as I imagined. My only companion was a rainstorm that happened to keep me company for about 100 miles. As we parted company, I thanked it for the music and pleasure it had brought me. I was alone and yet crowded with images of those who had gone before me and those who would follow. By the end of those 2 days I knew myself a little better and liked what I had learned.

A few days later, a group of us gathered to ride from Oklahoma to Indianapolis. This ride had it's own flavor. As we started out, there was a feeling of anticipation. We had no goal in mind other than to ride until we got tired, maybe stopping somewhere around St. Louis for the night. As we got under way, breakfast was to be the first order of business. Once the was accomplished, our band headed east. Gas stops took a little longer, but everyone was glad for the break. The group traveled well together, each looking out for the other. Mistakes were generously overlooked and skilled maneuvers were applauded.

West of St. Louis, it was decision time. Try to find a reasonably priced motel or brave the St. Louis traffic at 5:00 and find something on the other side. The decision was made and fortune smiled on our group. In less than 30 minutes we were in Illinois with minimal traffic behind us. Our "5:00 St. Louis traffic" fears had been unfounded. A celebration dinner was in order and this was secured at the Blue Springs Cafe. Great food and if you have room, "foot high pie" for dessert. After washing down dinner with plenty of lemonade and iced tea, it was decided to go a little further. With a spectacular sunset in our rear view mirrors, we headed east once more.

And so it continued. A great night to ride and now a new goal. Home [after a week on the road, can there be a sweeter word?]. Ride a little. Stop for gas. Stretch. Ride a little. Stop for gas. Stretch. Each rider drawing strength from the others. One last stop for coffee. Lot's of laughter and bad jokes but we knew we had made it. Each of us had a feeling of accomplishment. We had won and were almost giddy with success. And we knew beyond any boubt we could not have done it alone. The strength of the group had become our own individual strength.

Two styles of riding. One reason. Discovery. You can learn a great deal about yourself on a bike. Alone or with others. Different lessons, but one common denominator. Pure enjoyment. Go Enjoy.

# Eternal Vigilance

Riding a motorcycle is a special gift that also requires special skills. Yes, one takes a test and hopefully is issued a license from the state, but this is only the beginning. Sharp riding skills require practice, practice, and finally more practice. Reading articles and watching videos are good ways to gather information and pick up a few pointers, but there is no substitute for practice.

I recently got some practice during a ride through southeastern Indiana with a few friends. Excellent roads, great weather, good friends. Does it get any better than this? I was in my own world with nothing to concern me. Just me and the road. Hold it, what's that bee doing on my gas tank lid? I'll just flick him off of it and .......... In the second it took to flick that bee, I was off the road. For the next 100-150 yards I was doing 60 mph with my feet out on my highway boards, riding a 2 foot gravel edge. To my right - trees, to my left - a 6"- 8" ledge of fresh pavement. I had no where to go but forward. Ahead was a driveway with a smaller ledge enabling me to slam my front wheel onto it and pull my bike back onto the roadway. I remember thinking "I'm going down." and then "Not without a fight". This off road excursion lasted only 8-10 seconds, but it seemed like an hour. Never had I ridden so alertly, so consciously, so concentrated. Everything I'd heard about off road riding came back to me. Ride it, don't fight it. Don't lock the front brake. Look where you want to go. Once back on the road I found I could breathe again. A quick comment on the CB confirmed things were getting back to normal.

What happened ? What caused this "ride of terror "? Simple. Pilot error. Pure and simple. I had gotten complacent on a curve. Instead of paying attention to the upcoming apex, I was watching the countryside. Instead of feeling the ride, I was feeling the "ride" . A moment's diversion and my wife could have been a widow. Not a pleasant thought for either of us.

Sometimes the incident comes looking for you. That van making a sudden left turn, that patch of black ice, the deer bounding out of the woods, the ladder falling out of the truck in front of you, and so many more. We face enough challenges each and every time we mount up. We certainly don't need to tempt fate by making stupid mistakes or taking any unnecessary risks. The enjoyment, the relaxation, the peace we savor while riding is a very special and unique gift that so may others will never understand. Don't allow a momentary distraction to rob you of that gift. The lack of vigilance can demand a very high price. I pray none of us ever have to pay it.

# ANTICIPATION

OK, you've decided to go. 4 days at the Rally, 1 day to get there, 1 day to get back. 6 days of just you and your bike. You're already excited and the Rally isn't scheduled to start for another 2 months. What to do, what to do?

Let's start with the bike. Tires look good, oil was just changed, cables are fine, brakes are OK, battery's fully charged, lights are all in order. It's ready. Great, that killed 30 minutes. Just 59 1/2 days to go.

Routes. Yeah, routes. What's the best one to take? You grab your atlas and various state maps and for the next 4 hours, you're plotting distances, mileages, gas stops, motels, alternate routes ( just in case), and any other map related information you can squeeze out of a road atlas. Alright, 1 day down - 59 to go.

You don't want to get overzealous about this trip, so for the next month or so you tend to push it aside and concentrate on your day to day life. Go to work, pay some bills, catch a game. You try not to think about "the Rally ", but it keeps sneaking up on you. That bike on the interstate. It was pretty heavily loaded. Surely you can do better than that. That outdoor catalog you got in the mail. Do you camp at the Rally or play it safe and make those motel reservations? The TV commercial for American Express reminds you to check the credit limit on your charge cards. The evening news feature on highway repairs makes you think about what the road conditions will be at the Rally. As the weeks pass at the speed of a turtle on crutches, the day finally arrives. You get to turn the calendar in the kitchen. Only 3 weeks to go!!

Now you start thinking about packing. Not packing, prepacking. Mentally you pack, unpack, repack, unpack again, repack once more. OK you've got it. Now to put it on the bike. This mental feat alone will burn up 2-3 days. DAMN, you forgot your shaving kit! Now you have to mentally unpack again and repack all over again.

What, you've only got 8 days before you leave? Where did you put that travel bag last year? Where's your tank bag? The cassette tapes are in the car, aren't they? Who moved the tire gauge from the workbench? Gotta remember to pick up another can of spray cleaner. Cargo net looks a little frayed, doesn't it? Better get a new one just to be sure. Surely that old rainsuit's got another season left in it. Better check it, too. A new visor for your helmet wouldn't be a bad idea either since you're going to the bike shop anyway.

Since you're leaving tomorrow, you've made arrangements to leave work early today. As in taking the day off. By now you've packed twice and still haven't gotten it quite right. It was so much simpler 3 weeks ago. Finally you get it together and start loading up. Don't get upset - you knew you should have bought that new cargo net. Get the visor this time, too. Finally the bike is ready. You decide to give it a shakedown ride and go fill the gas tank. Duct tape should hold that body panel together until you can order a new one next week. You knew better than to anchor that bungee cord there anyway and when the load shifted, there wasn't anything you could do. By

11:00 PM you've finally reloaded the bike and feel confident that everything will stay put. Besides, you have to be up at 5:30 to leave by 6:00, so you really don't have much choice.

It's 4:45AM and you can't sleep. Today's the day. Reach over, turn the alarm off, get up, and let the adventure begin. It's been a long time coming.

One other thing. If your wife is going with you the whole process is much, much simpler. You buy a trailer and a whole bunch of prepaid UPS shipping labels. Believe me, you're gonna need 'em.

# A DIFFERENT CONVERSATION

"Steve."

What was that?

"Steve, yeah you."

Yeah you? I thought I was alone in the garage. At least I had been for the past couple of hours. My wife was out and I figured I could take advantage of the time to clean off my workbench and just generally clean the place up. No one had stopped by and I had been quietly enjoying my solitude.

"Quit acting like you don't hear me and turn around here."

I whirled around to see I was still the only person there.

"Who's there?" I said.

"Nobody but us fools, you fool" came the answer.

I looked around my surroundings. No one was there. Just me, the garage clutter, and my bike. Even the dogs were out back.

"Now you're starting to get it."

"Get what?' I answered a bit shaken.

"It, brainiac. Turn the volume down a bit on my stereo will you? I really prefer a quieter conversation instead of shouting, don't you?"

No, this isn't possible. The voice was coming from the speaker system on my Goldwing. In a daze, I stumbled over and lowered the volume as requested. At the same time, I removed the key from the ignition. Surely I was imagining this whole thing. Maybe I needed some coffee. Yeah, take a break and get some coffee. That's the ticket.

"Have all the coffee you want but don't lose that key. We're going to need it later."

OK, no coffee.

"This can't be real can it?" I said aloud.

"The way you handle me on certain occasions, I've often thought that myself." came the answer.

"And just what is that supposed to mean?" A talking bike was one thing, but one with an attitude was another matter.

"Don't be so smug. Do you really think I want to go out in 10 degree weather? Or in a driving rain? Or when you just let me sit for a couple of months? How about when you want to feel macho and push me to hard thru the curves? Sometimes I really wonder about you."

"Oh, so you don't think I'm qualified to pilot you about, huh?" Now I was getting a little warm. Real or not, my riding style isn't that bad and I usually ride when I want to, not when someone says it's ok.

"OK, ok, calm down. I'll grant you you're better than a lot of the other riders I've heard about. Not as good as some but better than others."

"And just what do you base this comparison on since only 3 other people have ever ridden you?" Gotcha, I thought.

"Give me a break. Do you think while you and your buddies are stuffing your faces on Sunday mornings, we're just sitting out on the parking lot killing time? You'd be amazed and surprised at the conversations we've had. Did you know that none of us appreciate being left dirty after a long ride?"

"You talk to each other!!" Maybe I needed something a bit stronger than coffee.

"Of course we do. Just because we chose not to talk to you riders doesn't mean we don't talk to each other."

"Thank you so much for lowering your standards to enlighten me about such things," I quipped.

"See, there you go again. Relax. Most of us are quite pleased with our riders. You're kinda like kids to us. Usually fun to be around, but occasionally in need of a little guidance."

"Guidance? You think we need guidance" Now my curiosity was peaked "please elaborate."

"Ok, I shall. Take notes, there will be a quiz later" came the sarcastic answer.

"Alright, let's hear these pearls of wisdom." Like this machine could really teach me anything I thought.

"When's the last time you checked my front fork air pressure smart guy?"

"Well, Ah,er..."

"How about my tire pressures?"

"I meant to do that later."

"You mean later as in later this year or later this century?"

"Hey now, theres no reason to be snooty about this."

"Battery levels come to mind. Perhaps lubing clutch and brake cables would be a fun past time. Once around the lights would be nice, too. How about an oil change?"

"Hold on a minute, I changed your oil just 800 miles ago, even put on new oil filter, too!" I exclaimed.

"Two points for the creature with opposing thumbs. How about a new air filter? Maybe a fresh fuel filter, too? New sparkplugs makes a great birthday gift. What the heh? Why not just go crazy and go for new plug wires at the same time. Maybe you could check the tire tread depth just for grins. How about those bolts just behind my headlight? Think we shoud tighten them or go on a scavenger hunt later? You really don't use my brake pads? You only need them to stop. The words "final drive fluid" ring a bell? How about "engine coolant"? Ok try "antifreeze". Read any good books lately? Like my owner's manual? You should hear some of the things my buddies say about chain tension and lubrication. Downright terrifying, if you ask me."

"Ok, ok, you've made your point," I stammered, "give me a break. I'm only..."

"Human? Yeah I know. Lord, do I know. You riders like to brag about your skills and prowess to each other, or anyone who'll listen for that matter, but how many of you brag about the care you give us? Not many I'll bet."

"Well after all, you're only a machine. Right?'

"Right. A machine that you depend on to bring you home safely from a 500 mile ride. A machine to transport you away from your day to day worries and woes. A machine that separate you from the average motorist. A machine that gives you a sense of pride, of purpose, of freedom, of completion. Ever wonder why you've never had a bad ride, regardless of destination or weather? I could tell you."

"No need, I think I understand, or at least I'm beginning to." I answered.

"I believe that maybe, just maybe, you do," the voice now had a more soothing tone about it." Do me a favor."

"Sure"

"I understand we can't ride everyday. No big deal, but when you pass by me in the garage, give me a light pat on the grip or saddle. It'll do us both good. And pass the word to your buddies. We'll make you a deal. You take care of us and we'll take care of you. Simple. One more thing. When you guys are "kicking tires", be kind. We don't dwell on your expanding "spare tires" during our parking lot visits."

"Ok, but why don't you bikes tell us yourselves? I'm sure all of us would love to hear from you."

"We have tried to talk to you with worn tires and frayed cables. Some of you just don't listen. If you ignore these things, why would you listen to a voice? Particularly one coming from a machine? Besides, it took 3 years for you to hear me. Most of us are traded off by then and we have to start again from scratch. Tell you what, the next time we're gathered together, you start the conversation and I'll chime in."

"You expect me to start talking to you out loud in front of my friends? Some of them already question my mental state. That's all the proof they'd need to lock me up." There's no way this conversation was going anywhere, I thought to myself. No one would believe me anyway.

"You don't want to talk to me, but you expect me to talk to them, right?"

"Right".

"That'll happen when BMW's and Harley's have interchangeable camshafts. Oh yeah, that'll happen."

I could have sworn the right signal winked at me.

# THE QUIET TREASURE

Recently, a friend of mine was involved in a mobile confrontation between his motorcycle and a pick-up truck. Obviously, we all know who got the worst of the deal. Fortunately, my friend came through the incident with only minor scratches and some discomfort. His bike? Well, it's always fun to look for a new ride especially using someone else's insurance money. The main point here is bikes are replaceable, friends are not.

During this incident a few riding buddies were pressed into service in various forms. Companion, communication coordinator, chauffeur, confessor, confidant, a number of things, or maybe just one - friend. Simple, direct, honest, no pretense, no games, one word that says it all.

Friend. A phone call I recently received was ended with "I'll talk to you later my friend." Not "Goodbye "or "See you around," but with "my friend." I could feel those two words wrap around me like an old comfortable sweater. I have driven 200 miles at 2:00 in the morning to help a friend. Even more incredible was the fact that I was accompanied by a friend who had already ridden 300 miles that day. But the real topper is the absolute fact that both of us would do it again without hesitation or question. Why? To help a friend. That's all the reason a friend needs and that's enough.

A friend can see you at your worst and tell you that you look your best. More often than not, you'll believe it. A friend can convince you that regardless of how lost you think you are, you're really only slightly misplaced. Is there any better sight than a friend carrying a thermos of coffee and smiling as he's walking toward you on a cold rainy night in the middle of nowhere after you've called him because your bike is dead? With his arrival the fear and apprehension simply vanish. Your friend's here, so everything is going to be fine.

I have made new friends and lost old friends. I have lost new friends and kept old friends. Thru it all, I have learned one constant truth. To have true friends, you have to be one. There are shortcuts, no quick fixes, no instant results. Friendship is like a garden. You can't leave it unattended or weeds will take it over. Every so often, you have to chase a varmint out of it. Of course, it takes faith and trust. In the end, you only get out of it what you put into it.

Do yourself a favor. Take a moment and tell your friends how you feel about them. It may be a bit uncomfortable at first, but do it anyway. They'll benefit from it and so will you. Remember, none of us really know what's around that curve up ahead or if that truck is going to make a hard left right in front of us. Once fate intervenes, you can't call for a time out to plan that last ride with your friends, but they'll be taking their first ride without you afterwards. Make sure your friendship goes with them and stays with them and that they can wrap your spirit around them. Kinda like an old comfortable sweater on a cold winter night.

# THE LEGACY

There should be a light or something. Isn't that what people say--a warm light, or a soft voice, or music, or something. Why can't I see anything ?

"Grandpa? Grandpa, can you hear me? "

Of course I can hear you.

"Grandpa, please say something."

I'd like to child, but I'm so tired. Seems easier to lay here and rest than to talk. I do wish you'd quit crying so much, though. This whole thing seems to be upsetting you a lot more than it is me.

"Come on Willie. Let Grandpa rest now. "

No, wait a minute, Willie.

" Mom, he's holding my hand. Let me stay. Please? Just another minute. Please?"

" Alright, but just for a minute. And be quiet.

Atta boy, Willie. You always were one of my favorites, even if I never told you so. I'd like to tell you now, but I'm so tired. Maybe later. Right now, just sit here with me a minute or so. Soon we'll both feel better about things.

"Grandpa, I know you're going away soon."

It's called dying Willie. Don't be afraid to say the word, boy. It won't hurt you. It's a fact of life. You're born, you die. Simple as that.

"Grandpa, remember the ducks? The ones on the pond? I do. I always will."

Yes Willie. I remember. That morning flight coming in and gently gliding down, was something very special between us. I remember the look of wonder in your eyes, the smell of the pine trees, the sound of the breeze in them, the feel of the grass beneath my feet. I remember it all. Odd, I remember it clearly, too. As though it was only yesterday, instead of so many years ago. I wonder why.

"I remember squirrel hunting, too Grandpa. The way you taught me to search the leaves for a tuft of fur, or the movement on a limb."

Do you remember how I almost had to shoot your first squirrel for you, too? How I had to sight the varmit in the scope and point it out to you? You were a game rascal then, Willie. You'd hunt on the worst day, never see a rabbit, never fire a shot, come home half frozen, and ask how soon you could go out again. How you loved the outdoors. Hunting or fishing, it made no difference. You would always want to go. Did I ever tell you how proud I was of you the day you put that bass back. Probably the biggest bass you'll ever catch, and you released it. Said you wanted someone else to enjoy catching him as much as you did. I've fished over 60 years Willie, and I've never known a finer moment.

" You saved my life once, Grandpa. When that house was on fire. I went up the stairs to see if anyone was there and sat down on a stair because I couldn't breathe. The next thing I knew, you were carrying me off the stairway. I was always amazed how much strength you had at that moment. I feel so helpless now. I wish I could do something."

Willie, no damned fire was going to get you. Not while I was around. Now it's different. There's nothing you can do for me. It's time for me to die and I know it. It's hard to accept, but once you do, it's not as terrible as you think. It's hard to leave you and everyone behind, but when you realize you don't have much choice in the matter, it seems somehow easier. I guess what really matters is what you leave behind, not who. I wish I could explain it to you, but it's so hard to speak right now. I only hope you know what I mean.

"Grandpa, I don't know if you can hear me or not, but I want to tell you something. Everytime I hunt or fish, you'll be with me. Everytime I cast a rod or shoulder a gun, I'll remember you You gave me a wonderful world to explore and I promise I will. My children will, too Grandpa. I promise. What did you call it? A legacy ? My legacy. Sunrises, thunderstorms, morning rain, clouds, snow, how to whittle, motorcycles, coffee in a thermos, good dogs, all of it. I'll cherish it all. I promise. I love you Grandpa. "

" Come on, Willie. It's over. "

" He heard me Mom. I know he did. "

"How do you know Willie?'

"Look Mom. See, he's smiling. "

# Summer Rides and Aliens

Long days, short nights, warm breezes. I once heard "If this ain't heaven, then I ain't going." Seems to fit this time of year. Whether it's a long day in the saddle or a short jaunt to the dealer to kick tires, there's something special about being out and about right now. Solo, two up, meeting with friends, or a solitary cruise, summertime riding just can't be beat.

Do you know how to tell if you live next door to a motorcycle rider? Tall grass in the yard, weeds in the garden, dirty gutters, windows that need washing, house in need of painting, all signs of the 2 wheeler's creed, "If it's nice enough to work outside, it's nice enough to ride."

My long-suffering wife, Angie, can (and has) testified to witnessing my possession by unseen forces once the temperature climbs above 70 degrees. I've gotten the mower out of the shed, gassed it up, went by the garage, and the next thing I know, I'm cleaning bugs off my Gold Wing's windshield.

Not only did I claim to have a 10 hour memory gap, possibly caused by alien abduction, but those rascally aliens put 350 miles on my bike as well! And not one of them was thoughtful enough to cut the grass for me! In their defense, they did fill the gas tank before returning the bike to my garage. Probably in the name of intergalactic peace or some such thing.

Riding my Wing is always a treat, but riding it in summer is about as pure as it gets. No bulky layers, no plugging in electric vests, or monitoring falling temperatures. Black ice hazards are but a memory. Instead, you look forward to the cooling temperatures of evening and the fading brilliance of sunset.

Another of summer's treats are the rallies. There's a rally every weekend somewhere, and, regardless of where you live, I bet there's at least one within reach. These rallies are great places to check out accessories in use. And if you're visiting the vendors, you might as well plan on taking some extra cash. If you can escape their sirens call financially unscathed, well, you're a better man than I. But, hey, that's what all that extra luggage on my Gold Wing is for, right? If not, there's always UPS. Just be sure to get home before your package arrives. It's tough to present a good defense if you're not there to do it in person.

Have you ever noticed that late summer rides seem more relaxed than other rides? Maybe it's because you know that tomorrow will be as nice as yesterday, and next week will give you the same great weather that you're enjoying today. Perhaps it's the laid back pace that goes hand in hand with rides to your favorite ice cream stand or watering hole. Or maybe it's the fact that Saturdays seem to start earlier and last a wee bit longer. Even a trip this time of year has a different feel to it. It doesn't have the sense of urgency that a spring trip does or the challenge of an early winter ride. Instead, a summer ride seems to have a slower, more relaxed feel to it. Almost as if the ride was saying "No rushing today. We're going just loaf along and see what we see. Might even smell a rose or two along the way."

Finally, remember that summer rides are fleeting things at best. Come January, you're going to need some good memories to get you thru that dark time. Just be sure to remove your key from your bike come winter. I don't know if those aliens have any experience on frozen roads. Besides, I'm not sure that an intergalactic license qualifies as a motorcycle endorsement.

# Riding With Murphy

Some days you can ride. Some days you can't. But even when I can't ride, I can still think about it. Planning future rides and reliving old ones is a favorite pastime of mine. And, as I get older, I'm finding that reliving the old rides can take up a fair amount of time. Why, with my Swiss cheese memory and skilled embellishment, I can make a 3 day ride last a week. Trouble is that no one wants to listen to me for 3 days, let alone a week. But I digress.

During one of these "mental rides", I came to the conclusion that even when I think I'm riding solo, I bring an unwelcome passenger along with me. His name is Murphy. As in "Murphy's Law." As in "If anything can go wrong, it will".

Ever throw on your chaps, zip up your jacket, strap on your helmet, put on your gloves, and mount up, only to find that your bike key is still in the right front pocket of your jeans? How about forgetting to repack your rain gear after letting dry overnight in the garage? Of course, you don't realize this until you've completely unpacked your bike looking for it while parked under an overpass waiting for a downpour to stop.

How about forgetting to lower your kickstand at a gas station or restaurant? Ever notice the size of the crowd watching as your bike slowly lays down on it's left side? Thinking back, I can't recall this event happening without an audience of at least 3 or more people, half of which are glad to help you right your steed because they've been there themselves. That kill switch ever mysteriously activate by itself? I mean, I didn't touch it and you didn't touch it. But after going thru an hour of mechanical cures and 6 phone calls to no avail, it dawns on you that maybe, just maybe, you might have bumped it the last time you got off the bike? You could almost hear Murphy chuckling in the distance.A friend of mine attended Daytona Bike Week and shot some of the most "colorful" pictures he'd ever taken. At least, he would have if he had remembered to put the film in the camera instead of leaving it on his bike, parked eight blocks away. Another buddy of mine tries to attend at least three rallies a year. He makes his plans, plots his routes, checks for motels, gets his bike ready, does everything one can do to prepare. And every year, he makes it to maybe one event. When asked about this, he smiles and simply says, "Blame Murphy".

When it comes to my own rally attendance, I've brought home an untold number of commemorative T-shirts over the years. But I don't have much of a collection. Once the event is over and the shirt is no longer available, the one I brought home mysteriously shrinks to a diminutive size that only my wife can wear. I keep buying T-shirts, hoping that these phenomena will stop. In the meantime, my darling wife, Angie, is accumulating quite a collection herself.

It doesn't seem to mater how many times I check the batteries in the flashlight I keep on my bike, or how long they've been in there. A week, a month, a year, it makes no difference.  fail, the moment I start to use the flashlight, the batteries  fade and the light goes dim as I use it. Unless of course, I'm doing something that's delicate or has me laying on my back on wet pavement. Then, the light goes out completely.

We all know checking your bike's fluid levels, lights, brakes, tires, and so on should be part of any preride ritual. While I am guilty of not performing these tasks on a regular basis, at least they are more than an annual event for me and my bike. On the other hand, some folks think that a spring tune up is enough maintenance for the entire year. These are the riders who's bikes I am usually working on when my flashlight dies. Usually without the best of tools. And  usually, just before it starts to rain with no shelter in sight.

When it comes to directions, Murphy still wants to be in charge. Even Lewis and Clark asked the Indians for help, and they traveled a heck of a lot farther than I do. They obviously had no problem asking for directions. So why is it that I hear this little voice in my ear saying "Directions? We don't need no stinking directions!" every time I get the urge to ask for some local help? If I've passed to same farmhouse 3 or 4 times, good sense may win out, and I might stop and as for some directions. If not, my laps may be interrupted by the folks who live there waving me in for a pit stop and asking me if I'm gaining on the leader.

Tucking a few $20.00 bills in your bike can be a real life saver. Not all motels and diners take plastic. And  even those that do can be attacked by electronic gremlins (Murphy's cousins, I believe) at the most inopportune times. If you've ever gone over your budget at a rally and home is 3 tanks away, you may be surprised at the sudden lack of credit card friendly establishments along the way. I've never had to use any of my twenties, but I know that as soon as I dip into my stash, Murphy will be right there waiting.

Another thing that wise guy Murphy's always doing is peeking over my shoulder, whispering that I'm to old to be doing this, and suggesting that I grow up. Well, I say no! Don't grow up. You can grow old with grace and wiser with time, but that's it. I know 65 year old "kids" who have never grown up and don't intend to. And they're the ones that give Mr. Murphy fits. The more he throws at them, the better they like it. They know there's a new adventure waiting for them around  the corner, around the next curve. And now matter how much he bellyaches or grouses or grumbles, that ol' lawmaker Murphy can't get in the way of their enjoyment.

Well, here's mud in your eye, Murphy. I'm going to take those $20 bills out of my bike and wave them in your face and then use them to take my wife to dinner. What do you think about that! Let the chips fall where they may.

# A LESSON TO BE LEARNED

Yes, thought the old men, it'll be a fine week-end for the hunt. All week he had been fretting about the weather for the upcoming hunt. Now it was Thursday night and the radio had just said that frost warnings would be in effect for the next 72 hours. Yes sir, thought the old man, frost and quail hunting go together like scotch and soda.

"James." bellowed the old gentleman. "You've made all the reservations like I told you, didn't you?"

"Of course, sir, " replied James, coming into the room. "The plane leaves at 7:43 and arrives at 10:29. Your usual room is already prepared and breakfast will be served as usual at 4:00. You should easily be in the field by dawn tomorrow.

"And my bags? "

"Packed and ready, sir."

"Very well James, let's be at it."

Walking over to the gun cabinet, the old man paused a moment. The rich mahogany gleamed and was smooth to his touch. The Purdey or the Parker, mused the old man. Picking both up, he smiled quietly to himself. An over-and-under is hard to beat, the old man thought, but when ol' Bob started moving, the side by side Purdey seemed to have a mind of it's own. Maybe next time, he thought, as he gently placed the Parker into it's own special resting place. The light from the fireplace danced over the rich, dark wood of the gun cabinet and the still darker barrels of the many guns it contained. The old man looked at the image for but a moment, then turned and left.

The flight was uneventful, although it seemed never to end. The hotel limousine picked him up at the airport as arranged and by 11:30, the old man was dreaming of a large pointer, frozen in a heart-stirring point.

Morning rolled around and breakfast was served. Half-dozen of eggs, poached, four pats of sausage, two pieces of toast, lightly buttered, one stack of cakes with honey, hash browned potatoes, and three cups of coffee, black--the same breakfast he had on the opening day of quail season for the past 43 years, and in the same room where he had that breakfast for that many years.

"Can't do a decent days' hunting on an empty stomach," he said to the maid as she removed the tray.

"Seems to me you should be able to hunt for about a week or so after that kind of breakfast" came the reply.

"Huh," said the man after the door had shut. "Seems nobody approves of a decent breakfast anymore."

The knock came on the door just as the man had finished lacing the boots, which had been freshly broken in just for this trip.

"Come in if you're going to" he snorted.

A lean, drawn looking youth opened the door and shyly walked on.

"Who are you?" inquired the old man, with the look of a hawk inspecting a mouse.

"I come to see if you need a guide. I mean, you need a guide and Dave Johnson busted his leg a couple of weeks ago, and I thought maybe....."

"Johnson did what!!!" roared the old man.

"Busted his leg, sir" answered the boy. Something about this man demanded the "sir ". "Out breakin' in some new dogs and his horse shied at something, and threw him and it busted."

"Why the hell didn't he call me? He's known I would be coming, for months. "The old man was really getting worked up now. Forty-three years and he had never missed an opening day. Forty-three years. Why, even back in ' 42, with the war going on, he'd always made it. And even in ' 54 he'd been here instead of New York at the merger of two of his companies. Why, to miss the opening day was unthinkable, and now, the best guide in four states was laid flat on his back with a "busted" leg.

"Sir," this voice seemed to say, "I know how far you've come and how much you like to hunt, and I thought that maybe I could guide you, that is if that's alright by you. I know someplace's that might have a few quail in 'em and they ain't too hard to get to and...."

"Boy, are you saying I can't get around as well as I used to? " bellowed the man. "Let me tell you something. I was hunting quail before were even a thought in your father's head, and for that matter, before he was a thought in his father's head. And I'll still be hunting quail when your son has thoughts of sons. If there's one thing I'll not tolerate, it's some young babe-in-the-woods thinking I'm old and decrepit and should have been put out to pasture a long time ago. Do you understand me boy?"

"Yes sir," smiled the boy. "sir, my name ain't boy. It's Charlie, Charlie Peters."

"Alright bo... Charlie. You got any references?"

" References? What's references?"

"References!! Someone who'll vouch for you and your ability in the field, "stormed the old man.

"Well sir," drawled Charlie, "I don't go hungry."

The man thought a moment. "Well Charlie, I guess you got a point there" he said at last. "You got any dogs?"

"Well sir, I can only afford one, and even then only because I found her as a pup. But she'll find birds, alright. She really enjoys her work. She ain't all that much to look at, but I'm happy with her."

Great, thought the man, I'm going to have to spend opening day with a kid who thinks he can hunt and his two-bit, flea-ridden hound.

"And what do you have to shoot with, Charlie?"

"I've got an old 12 gauge, single shot Stevens."

"You hunt quail with a single shot? " questioned the old man, staring Charlie straight in the eyes.

The answer and stare came right back.

"I make do."

"Alright Charlie, I'll be honest with you. It's too late to try and find another guide, and I'm not about to go back home, so you got yourself a client. One condition, however, I'll pay you at the end of the hunt, whatever I deem proper. Agreed?"

"I reckon I can trust you to be fair" said Charlie, " so I agree." Extending his hand he said, "When would you like to leave? "

Shaking hand, the man replied, " soon can you be ready ? "

"I'm ready now sir. My gun and Queenie is already? "

"Then let's be at it."

Two and a half hours later, the truck finally came to a grumbling halt. After careful inspection to be sure that all of his parts were where they were supposed to be, the man lumbered down from the truck. How he had hated to put the fleece-lined case, that contained the Purdey, in the bed of the old truck. Only after he'd taken it out of it's custom fitted case and felt it in his hands could he finally breath a sigh of relief. All his fears were unfounded. It had been as safe and comfortable as if it had been in that mahogany gun cabinet, hundreds of miles away.

"Mighty fine gun you got there, sir," said Charlie, getting down from the truck, gun in hand.

"One of the finest ever made," came the reply.

"I believe it," said Charlie as he got Queenie down from the bed of the pick-up. The man thought he detected a slight note of awe for a moment, but then it was gone.

"Kind of late to get a start, isn't it?" asked the old man.

"Never did meet a quail that wore a watch," grinned Charlie, rough housing with Queenie for a moment. "Course, I ain't met all of 'em yet. Queenie, get yourself out there and find this nice gentleman some quail. Mind you, if you see any with pocketwatches, you let me know first." With this said, Charlie winked down at Queenie and sent her to work.

For a moment, the old man could have sworn the dog winked back.

"Enough of this foolishness," he sputtered, " I come here to hunt quail, not listen to some kid play games with a dog. Are you going to hunt birds or sit on that truck all day? "

"I'll do some huntin' if it's all the same to you, sir" replied Charlie, turning serious. "Being as you're the guest, you should take the first shots."

"Alright, I'll shoot first, but you are not to shoot, regardless of my results. I'm wise to the kind of pressure you can put on a man. Might make him shoot too soon, and then you've got a simple straight-away shot. We'll rotate first shots. Agreed?"

"Ok by me," answered Charlie, "just trying to be polite."

While the man was loading the loops on his jacket with #8 shot, he had an eye on Charlie, who was doing something the man didn't quite understand. Charlie would pick up a shell from a bag he carried them in, look at it a moment, then put it in a pocket in his pants. Some shells would go in one pocket, some in another.

"What in the hell are you doing, Charlie?"

"Sorting shells, sir."

"What ? "

"Sorting shells, sir. #8's go in my right pocket, #6's in my left."

"#6's on quail, Charlie ? Kinda large, isn't it? "

"Not always, sir. "

All during this time, Queenie had been about her business, and now she was down to serious business.

"Reckon we outa join her" said Charlie.

Slipping two shells into the Purdey, the old man slowly approached the statue of a dog. Helluva point, he thought, as he crept by her. Then, all creation broke loose. He was in the middle of a brown and white thunderstorm. There was no rain, but more thunder than he remembered. But the old man was no birds' fool, and brought down two of the small, brown thunderbolt.

"Nice shooting," cried Charlie. "Queenie, if you'll do the honors, we'll get back to business again."

And honors they are, thought the old man. The dog returned each bird with a style that seemed to say, "It's my privilege to bring these birds back to you. Please accept them with my gratitude."

"Charlie, you ever thought about selling this little lady? I'm sure you could get a handsome price for her."

"No sir, I'd never thought much about it. Don't reckon I'll ever sell her. She's more than just a dog to me," said Charlie quite soberly.

"I think I understand," said the old man. For a moment, he and Charlie stared at each other, and Charlie believed he did understand.

Queenie had "frozen" again and Charlie got ready to do his part. Quietly he slipped a shell from his right pocket into the old Stevens and then held a shell from his left pocket between the second and third fingers of his left hand.

"What in the hell are you doing? " questioned the old man. But he never received a verbal answer.

Charlie had stepped into the same thunderstorm as the old man had moments earlier, and it happened. The man saw it as though it were happening in slow motion. The quail rose, Charlie sighted, shot, ejected the spent shell; reloaded, sighted, and shot again. The old man was speechless.

"Queenie, if you'll do the honors."

Queenie scurried out and retrieved one bird. Dropping it in Charlie's outstretched hand, she raced out and brought back the second.

Words came back to the old man.

"That's impossible!!! I mean, it can't be done. Nobody can get a double with a single-shot. It's just impossible!!!"

"I don't mean to call you a liar sir, but when a body's got four brothers and three sisters to feed, well he can't waste much time shootin' single birds."

"What ? You mean to tell me you always get doubles with that gun of yours?"

"Oh no sir. Most of the time, but not always, "grinned Charlie, "sometimes I gets three birds."

"Triples !!!"

"Sometimes, sir. Found that I can hunt half as long that way, and still get enough to go around."

"Charlie, how old are you?"

"Seventeen, sir."

"How long have you been doing that?"

"Doing what, sir?"

"Scoring doubles, damn it!!"

"Bout three years."

"You were shooting doubles with a single-shot at the age of fourteen!"

"Yes sir."

"I'll be damned. I'll be a ringtailed jackass. That's got to be the most unbelievable shooting I've ever seen, and sometimes you get triples. The boys back home will never believe this. Triples with a single-shot."

"Sir, if you're ready, we'd best get busy. Queenie seems to be standing mighty still over by that clump of bushes. Sure looks like she's inviting us over for a mighty good reason."

The old man looked over in her direction, and sure enough, the little black and white setter wasn't so much as breathing loudly. One front paw crocked in the air and her tail pointed straight to the heavens. Her whole being seemed to say, "Any time you're ready, gentlemen."

"Charlie you take this shot."

"No sir, it's your shot, fair and square."

"Charlie, you take this shot. Remember, you've got a family to feed. I'll just stand back and watch. "

"Well sir, it you insist."

"I do."

Putting a shell from his right pocket into the old Stevens once more, and a shell from his left pocket in is left hand, Charlie came alongside Queenie once more. And again it happened. Quail rose, Charlie sighted, shot, ejected the spent shell; reloaded, and shot again. And again, the old man was speechless.

Queenie retrieved both birds with superb grace and style. Charlie thanked her with a loving pat on the head, turned to his hunting companion and asked if he would like some lunch.

It was all the old man could do to nod.

On the way back to the truck, the old man was strangely quite.

"Have I done something to upset you, sir?" asked Charlie.

"No, I was just thinking about your shooting this morning," the old man replied.

"Did I do something wrong? "

"Oh no, Charlie. I doubt if anyone could find any fault with your shooting this morning. Charlie, let me ask you something. Why do you hunt?"

" That's easy. For food. "

" That's it ? "

" That's it. I take enough birds to feed the family. We ain't got much money and it stretches a lot farther if I bring in some birds or rabbits or squirrels. I don't take more than we need, since it don't make sense to waste what the good Lord put here. "

"Couldn't you get more game with a better gun? "

"Maybe, maybe not, " said Charlie, glancing down at the Purdey the old man was carrying. "Gotten sorta used to this one, you know? "

"Yeah, I know what you mean," answered the older, and perhaps wiser of the two.

Thus it went on, for three days. Charlie making the impossible look easy, and the old man becoming more and more humble and quiet, around him. Those who had known the old man from seasons past, couldn't understand the change that had come over him, nor did they try. To most of them, he was "the rich old man from the city" and that's all he would ever be.

At last, Sunday night came and it was time to pay the wages to the boy who had done the impossible.

"Charlie, sit down in that chair and don't say a word until I've finished," ordered the old man.

Charlie sat and waited. Everyone had told him not to out-shoot the old man, but he had argued that he shot only for the food, not for the sport of it. Now he wondered if he had done the right thing. Maybe he should have missed a few on purpose. No, shells are too expensive to waste. He had done the right thing.

"Charlie, in the past 43 years I have hunted with hundreds of men. Some of them have been damn good shots and others couldn't hit the broad side of their own broad-sides, with either hand. But, in all my years of hunting, I have never had the honor or privilege of spending so much time in the field with a more pleasant knowledgeable hunting companion and sportsman. I have seen more quail in the past three days than I have seen in three years, but more important than that, you have reminded me of myself many, many years ago. Not that I could ever have held a candle to your shooting abilities, but I too, loved the woods and fields in my younger days. And I have watched you and Queenie. That is no ordinary dog you've got there. She is an extension of yourself. And thus it should be, between a man and his dog. Charlie, what do you think a fair wage would be for your services these past few days?"

"Well sir, "replied Charlie,"I was thinking somewhere's around thirty dollars, or so".

"Really", answered the old man, "I was thinking of something different," as he laid three 100 bills on the table.

"That's settled," the old man paused a moment. "How about selling me that gun of yours, Charlie."

"What? Oh no sir, I couldn't do that. It's the only one I got and I gots to keep it."

"Well, how about trading?"

"Tradin' sir ? Tradin' what, sir? "

"My gun for your gun."

Now it was Charlie who was speechless. For the past three days he had dreamed of owning a fine shotgun someday soon. Maybe in time for next season. But a Purdey ! Him,Charlie Peters, owning the only Purdey for a hundred miles.

"Sir, you're only funnin', ain't ya?"

"No Charlie, I'm quite serious. Hurry up now, I've got a plane to catch."

"Well, er, a, yeah, sure, OK."

"Alright, it's a deal. I haven't cleaned it yet, so go over it good when you get it home. May as well take the case, too. Won't fit any of my other guns. Oh Charlie, would you mind driving me to the airport? I'm all packed and your truck is handier than anything else at the moment. Besides, it'll give me a chance to say good-bye to Queenie."

So they rode to the airport in the old battered truck, Charlie driving, the old man sitting quietly with Queenie between them, her head on the old man's lap.


Plans were made for next year's seasons, and promises made. The old man slept through the flight home and James picked him up at the airport. As usual, James had a late supper prepared and the old man ate in the den while James lit a fire in the large, but warm, fireplace. After supper, the old man sipped his bourbon by the fireplace and, occasionally, he would glance over to the mahogany gun cabinet and smile at the lights dancing off of the Parker over-and-under, and an old pitted single-shot Stevens, proudly standing beside it.

# FRIENDS AND MAGIC

The house was quiet, as well it should be, he thought. No reason for anyone else to be up at 4:15 in the morning. Some of the magic of the forthcoming hunt was taking place there at the kitchen table. Fumbling through the shotgun shells, fixing the extra sandwich, grabbing an apple from the icebox, sharpening the knife, lacing up the boots--all of this was just as important and just as mystical as trudging through the three inches of snow that had fallen that night. Some things are hard to explain, he mused. He found himself enjoying the quietness of his sleeping family and thought how, it too, was part of the magic.

"You're forgetting your thermos."

The sound startled him and he broke a bootlace as he looked up.

"No I'm not," he said. "I just haven't gotten to it yet."

"I'll do it," she said. "You know my coffee's better than yours anyway. You wouldn't want Dave to drink that rot-gut of yours, would you."

"It didn't kill him last time, did it? Of course, he does blame his getting skunked last trip on it, but that's not the real reason he didn't..."

"Tell me when you get home. That way you won't have to make up any fresh stories."

"Stories!! Me!" he exclaimed. Of course she was right. Odd how quickly she had caught on to his game. They had only been married a little over a year and this was her second hunting season with him. Yet, she seemed to understand his need to be "in the thick of it" as she called it. He was damn lucky to have her and he knew it. Of course, he couldn't let her know it. Not too often, anyway.

"I'll put the gear in the car, " she said.

"Are you crazy ? It's 18 degrees out there. I'll do it. Besides, I have to get Bagel yet, anyway. "

"I wish you wouldn't call him that."

"Well, it's your fault, you know. 'Cheese, bread, butter, beagles'-- that's what the list said. What else could I name my hunting dog. Bagel the beagle."

"His name is Sir Richard of the Golden Heart."

"Maybe on paper, but in the field or with me, it's Bagel. Besides, Bagel is a lot shorter and a helluva lot easier to use."

"Whatever. Do you want breakfast?"

"No thanks. If I get hungry, I'll stop and a grab bite."

"Promise?"

She was always worrying. "Promise." he said. "Now go back to bed."

The drive to Dave's normally took 15 minutes, but with the icy roads, it took him half an hour to get there.

"Strange. There's no lights on at Dave's house, Bagel 'ol boy. Oh well, he'd never forgive us if he didn't go with us on such a glorious morning." Upon saying such, the pair of them bounded up to the door of the darkened house.

"You in the house. This is the police. We have a warrant for the arrest of one, David Turner. Come out with your hands in plain sight. You have no place to hide. If you're not quite in 30 seconds, we will commence firing. Come out with your hands above your head."

"Good God in heaven Jim. Will you get off that doorbell and shut that miserable dog of yours up. I got to live in this neighborhood you know. It's 5 o'clock in the morning, for Christ's sake."

"And a lovely 5 o'clock it is, too. Why aren't you ready to go?"

"Didn't you hear the weather last night?"

"Yeah, what about it ?"

"Four to six inches of snow, low of 10 degrees, remember?"

"Yeah, great weather to be rabbit hunting. How quick can you get ready?"

"Give me 20 minutes," groaned David.

"You got 10."

"And if I'm not ready?"

"Bagel and I call for reinforcements."


Ten minutes later, the three of them headed out towards one of the few rabbit areas that still could be counted on.

"Coffee. I got to have some coffee," croaked David.

"It's in the thermos."

Poring himself a cup, he paused. "Who made it?"

"Just drink it," came the terse reply. "By the way, "you did remember to bring shells this time, didn't you?"

"Who knows? With you two on the warpath, I was lucky to grab my gun or coat, let alone shells."

"Well, I've got enough for both of us if needed, but when you strike out, don't be telling me there's no shot in yours."

"Then, by God, I'll choose which box mine come from."

"One small practical joke and you never live it down. You never minded using my handloads before. Have ye no faith? No confidence in my expertise at the loading bench? No belief in my basically good nature?"

"None whatsoever."

Finally, they arrived at their destination. While the field only covered 5 to 6 acres, the briars, rock piles, and tunnels, all made it a rabbet's idea of heaven. Unpacking the guns, the pair started along the fencerow, hoping to jump something quickly. Bagel was already hard at work, plowing through the small drifts like a miniature bulldozer. Jim off to the left and David hugging the fence. They had hunted together so often, it was second nature. Rabbit, quail, pheasant, squirrel -- it made no difference. They seemed to hunt as one. Same pace, same concern, same intensity, same joy.

"One up!" shouted David.

Before Jim could raise his gun, the brown blur disappeared down a tunnel.

"Getting a bit slow, are we? Maybe it's a little too chilly out here for your old bones," chided David.

"Your bones have 10 years on mine. Besides, I didn't see any blinding speed on your part," said Jim.

"I just thought I'd be polite and let you have the first one."

"David, do you see Emily Post out here anywhere ? Does this look the place to worry about which side the napkin goes on? Do you want to hunt or do you want to plan a tea party?"

"Right now I just want to keep warm"

"Then let's keep going."

Before David could respond, Bagel sang out. This was the part both men enjoyed most. Both had passed up shots on previous occasion, just to listen to the music of the beagle. Bagel's voice carried out over the snow covered field, crisp and clear. Both hunters could tell by the pitch of the sound how close the beagle was to it's quarry. Both instinctively knew who would shoot. Words were not needed, nor desired.

As Bagel brought the rabbit from behind a large rockpile, Jim's gun came to his shoulder, almost as if it had a life of it's own. His shot was true and a moment later, his game pouch was a couple pounds heavier.

"It must be nice," said David.

"What's that?" asked Jim.

"To own a dog that is smart enough and educated enough to find a rabbit who's time has come, and then to bring that same rabbit to you so you can look good. "

"What are you talking about?

"Hell Stevenson, you missed that rabbit by a good 3 feet. Good thing for you Bagel had worn it out so much that it had a coronary when it did. Like I said, you've got a damn selective dog there."

"At least my dog knows what to do around a rabbit. That mangy mutt of yours gets lost trying to find it's feed bowl. "

"Now let's not get out of line here. You can make fun of my wife or joke about my old shotgun, but don't be puttin' the finger on 'ol Jingle. In his time, he could have shown your hound a thing or two, or three for that matter." There was a touch of anger and pride in David's voice, but both men knew no offense had been meant. Besides, what's a friend for it if you can't razz him a little, every so often.

Their attention turned back to the business at hand, each quietly smiling to himself. This was the real reason they were here. Not to see how heavy their game bags could get, but rather how many memories could be gathered. During the heat of July the memory of cold hands on a cold gun would feel good. Washing the car in August can be done with rockpiles around, if you have the right memories. More than once, the blaring sound of a radio had drifted into a different music that had been shared by a more private audience. All a man had to do was know where to find it. For both men, it could always be found in the memory of a hunting trip. They knew there would be empty game bags, more often than not, but memories were always there to be gathered, stored and brought out every so often.

"Commin' at ya," shouted Jim.

David glanced ahead and saw the cottontail bouncing toward him. Throwing up his shotgun, he shot instinctively. The rabbit darted off to the left and was gone. He stared at it in disbelief. Shaking his head, he walked over to Jim, who was smiling, but being careful not to laugh.

"Give me you gun."

"What?"

"I said give me your gun, Stevenson."

"Why?"

"Stevenson, you low-lying, egg-sucking, fence-jumping, weasel. Give me your gun before I wrap this one around your neck."

Handing it over, Jim watched David unload both guns and put the shells from Jim's autoloader into his own pump. After putting the shells from his pump into the automatic, he handed it back to Jim, who was now roaring with laughter.

"I don't believe it! I can't believe it! Why don't your just admit you missed? Hell man, everyone does occasionally. When I missed those two last week, did I blame you? Of course not!! Admit you are but a mere mortal and subject to the weakness of the flesh!!"

"I seem to be more subjected when I use your shells."

"Well, if you had been ready on time, you wouldn't have to beg shells off me. Tell you what. We'll go back to the car and you can sort, shake, inspect, examine and pick any shell you want. That's fair isn't it?"

Now it was David's turn to smile. "Let's just keep going. I'll try to get by with these."

"But ..."

"No buts. There goes Bagel."

Sure enough, Bagel was bringing another rabbit towards the pair. This time, however, it was Jim's gun which sounded, to no avail.

"Oh well, you can't hit 'em all," said Jim.

David only smiled.

After about an hour and a half the trio found themselves at the end of the field. Bagel looked as if to say "Well let's go back through it one more time. I know there's at least one more in there," and as in answer to the unspoken challenge, the two hunters turned back towards the car.

"You know, " said Jim, " the easiest way back would be along that fencerow."

"And let you brag to that pretty wife of yours how you outshot me today!" cried David. "No way in hell. I'm going back the same way I got here, just as soon as I eat a sandwich and grab a coffee."

"What sandwich? What coffee?"

"That extra sandwich you always make. Now fork it over. And the thermos, too."

"Uh, Dave 'ol buddy," started Jim, "I'm not sure how to tell you this, but...."

"You didn't!! You couldn't!! You wouldn't!! Even if you did, tell me you didn't!!"

"Now Turner, calm down. It's not like it's the end of the world."

"It could be the end of yours."

"Now don't get crazy on me. The car's not that far, and besides, we're going that way anyway."

"The man gets me up at 5:00 in the morning," moaned David, rolling his eyes towards heaven, "wakes up half the neighborhood doing it, gives me empty shotgun shells to hunt with, and now he doesn't bring the thermos with him. Eighteen blessed degrees and he leaves the coffee in the car. Lord, I know you're busy, but when you strike him dead, bear in mind he deserves it. I'm sure everyone here will understand. Justifiable homicide, I believe it's called."

"Turner, do you want to pray or hunt?"

"I'll hunt. You start praying."

Bagel's cries cut off any response from Jim. At the sound, both men turned sharply towards the field and strained for any sight of the beagle. He was moving and moving quickly by the sound of him. Suddenly, a brown blur rushed out not 20 feet from David. Without raising his gun, David fired and watched the rabbit tumble. He then calmly strode over and stuffed the animal into his game pouch, all with the manner of someone walking to his kitchen and pouring himself a glass of iced tea.

"Now we can head back to the car," he announced.

Jim could only shake his head in amazement.

As they drove back to David's home, Jim was unusually quiet.

"You're not upset about me finishing off the coffee, are you?" inquired David.

"Of course not. That's what it was there for," laughed Jim. "I was just thinking about Jingle. How old is he now, anyway?"

"Oh, 11 or 12 by now, I'd say. Why?"

"That would make him around 80 to 90 years old if he were human, right?"

"Yeah, so?"

"Imagine hunting that long, David," answered Jim. "Imagine hunting all your life until you were just too old to be out any more. Until your bones simply couldn't take the cold, your eyes, once sharp, now faded. Your pace, once strong and sure, now feeble and slow. What would you do?"

"I don't know," came the somber reply. "guess I'd look back and wish I could start it all over again."

"Do you think Jingle does?"

"Of course. You've seen him asleep. The way he jerks, he's got to be dreaming of the old days. Hell, even his snoring sounds like he's hot on some rabbit's tail."

"Yeah, I suppose you're right."

With this, the car pulled into the drive. After unloading David's gear and receiving a stern warning about pulling such early morning wake-up stunts again, Jim started home.

It was about noon when Jim pulled into his own driveway. After putting his own gear away and rinsing out the thermos, he turned to his wife who was inspecting Bagel for any burrs that might need her attention.

"Sometimes I wonder why I bother." he started. "I mean, look at the money I spend hunting. That rabbit alone cost roughly 15 to 18 dollars by the time you figure the price of my gun, shells, coat, boots, gas, not to mention anything else. Look at the time it takes up, too. Why, just last season alone, I can remember a dozen times when I got home hours late. Hell, one time I didn't get home at all until the next day. Of course, it wasn't my fault the transmission went out in the middle of nowhere, but still, I was gone. And for what? To walk in 6 inches of snow with a cutting wind in my face, just to shoot an animal. Sure I like rabbit pie or squirrel stew, but I could live without them. Besides, what difference will it make 10, 20, 30 years from now. No one will care. No one will even know."

"I'll care, I'll know, "she replied.

"I know. But, what I mean is, why go at all?"

"Did you enjoy yourself today?" she asked.

"Of course, but...?"

"Did you enjoy David's company?"

"You know I did."

"Do you have another story to tell me about today?"

This time he smiled. "Well as a matter of fact..."

"Then stop and think. You've always said a good day is not measured by the weight of the bag, and I believe you. Everytime you're gone hunting, I know you're having a good time, regardless of the weather. You're always so excited before you leave and so happily tired when you come home, you always want to tell me something about each time you're out, and when you do, I can see the little boy in you. Think about everything involved with your hunting. Your guns, thermos's of coffee, snow, pre-dawn breakfasts, dogs, wind, the smell of gunpowder. I can tell you why you hunt, even if you can't. "

"You can?" he asked.

She smiled and simply said, "For the magic."

# THE STRANGER

I couldn't help but notice him as I was gassing up. He looked as if he was a stock item on the ST1100, rather than it's rider. Black boots, black chaps, black leather jacket, black gloves, black full face Shoei helmet all riding a black bike. Only the silver reflective halo on his helmet broke the color scheme. As I topped off my tank and walked over to pay the attendant, I politely smiled and nodded my head ' hello '. His response was merely a grin, although I sensed something more.

On my way back to my bike, I heard a voice say "been ridin' long?" I turned and answered "a few years now".

"I meant today" he replied.

"Oh, about 500 miles or so. Another 140 and I'll be home" I quipped.

"I'm not sure when I'll be home, but that diner over there is my next destination. Seems like forever since lunch. Feel like grabbing a bite with a fellow rider?"

I though for a moment. Just a couple of hours and I could be sitting in front of a warm fireplace and enjoying the feeling of being home. After a week on the road, that idea was uppermost in my mind. But there was something different about this guy and hot food did sound pretty good.

"Sure " I said "I'll go get us a table and meet you over there."

As I rode thru the parking lot I thought to myself, I must be crazy. I'm not really that hungry and every minute in the diner was a minute longer it would take to get home. Why had I agreed to this? Maybe I should just go on. After all, I would never see this guy again and even if I did I could explain my hasty departure one way or another. No, it was after 9:00 already and hot coffee and real food would be a good buffer against the cold dark road that lay ahead of me.

I went in, sat down, and ordered two coffees.

As the man approached the table I got a much better look at him. He carried his helmet in his left hand and as he gently sat it in the seat next to him I noticed a scar that ran up his forearm. His walk was slow but steady. His grey hair had been thinning out for a while I guessed. He wore no glasses, but did produce a pair to help read the menu. I would have guessed his height at about 5'9' to 5'10', but it was hard to tell as he shed his jacket and vest that was beneath it. The chaps remained in place. His watch looked expensive and I had a feeling that money was not a problem for him. His face was lined with a few wrinkles and had a straight forward look about it. He could have been anywhere between 40 and 60 years old. You knew just by looking at him, he was incapable of telling a lie. The truth was the only thing that face would allow to leave it's lips.

"Good coffee" he said.

"Figured we both could use some." I answered " How long have you been in the saddle?"

"Today?" he grinned.

"Yes, today" I grinned back.

"I left Philly at 6:00 this morning. With any luck I'll pull into my sister's house in Denver late tomorrow afternoon."

"That's over 1800 miles !!!" I exclaimed.

"Just a touch".

"What's the hurry? You know there's weather moving in from Oklahoma and Missouri tonight don't you? Might not be a bad idea to lay low and let it pass thru".

"Son, if I let a little storm stop me, I may as well sell the ST and buy a station wagon." I could tell he wasn't offended by my statement, but he wasn't concerned by it either.

"So, how many miles have you got on your ST?" I asked.

A look came over the face sitting across from me that made me feel like I had asked the teacher to repeat the lesson for the third time.

"Miles, huh? Well, this ST has a little over 130,000. My first one had over 200,000 when I traded her in. But miles aren't what your asking about, are they? You're really asking if I've "been there". Well sir, I've "been there" and then some, and I've relished every moment of it."

" Really," I replied "Tell me about some of your travels if you don't mind. I really would like to hear about them. At least this way we can get thru dinner quickly and I can get back on the road, I thought.

"How 'bout I tell you something important instead?" His response caught me off guard.

"Sure," I said, motioning to the waitress for more coffee.

"You don't know me and that's fine. I couldn't say these things if you did. A lot of people claim they know me, some even claim to be friends. But they don't know me, not really. I've enjoyed moderate success in the business world so I am fortunate that I can travel to the extent that I do. I know and am thankful that I'm luckier than most. My health is good. I quit smoking about 8 years ago and am a bit more choosey about what I eat now. I'm not a health fanatic, but I realize there's less road ahead of me than behind me.

I've been a lot of places since losing my wife a few years back. The Four Corners Run, Deals Gap, the Blue Ridge Parkway, Pacific Coast Highway, Spearfish Canyon, Highway to the Sun, Million Dollar Highway, Bear Tooth, Needles Highway, and countless others. Seems I can't sit still. Always seems to be another road to ride. My kids don't understand. They think I'm just running away from my memories. Maybe I am in one way or another. I don't know.

Sometimes it bothers me that no one really, truly, knows me. I want to be remembered. Not as the man who ran the Iron Butt 10 years in a row, but as the man who felt it was more important to help a fellow rider on the road than to win the race. It's important to me that somebody know how I cried at the simple beauty of a sunset in New Mexico, how I laughed when I dropped my bike at a gas station because I forgot to set the kickstand, how I tasted fear as I rolled over in my sleeping bag to see a rattlesnake less than 12 inches from my throat.

There are things that are deep and private to me which are not meant to be shared with just anyone. Even today with the cold weather, I couldn't wait to ride. Most people would never have left the garage. That's their loss. The feeling of being "on the road" is something that still excites me. The look of wonder on a child's face as you pass a car and wave to them. The feel of autumn on a back road. Being so hot you can't even sweat in the desert. Wondering if you'll ever be warm again as you ride thru the Rockies. Getting caught in a sudden summer downpour with lightening hitting the ground on either side of you and grinning the whole time. The game of trading bikes at your favorite dealer. The feel of your first new bike. Keeping a promise once made, even if no one else would ever know, simply because you said you would. Honor and integrity are still very much alive within me. Maybe it's just me, but I don't believe those qualities are as common as they once were.

To this day I still miss the guys I rode with 20 years ago. Some just quit riding, others just ran out energy, and a couple ran out of time. Their memories ride with me to this day and will always do so. I have to believe that where you've been is as important as where you're going. But it's not racking up miles on an odometer that counts. It's racking up the memories, feelings, sights, sounds, smells that truly count. What good is riding 300 miles if you have no adventure doing it? I tell you, I'd rather ride 50 miles with a true friend and share a thermos of coffee at a rest stop than do 500 mile for bragging rights.

Seems odd, doesn't it, that I can talk so freely with a stranger. Maybe I just needed to get some things off my chest. Maybe it's because I know that I've got some miles to ride before my journey ends and I needed some companionship. Maybe I just like to hear my own voice. "

"Maybe it's because I'm such a good listener" I joked.

"Maybe," he smiled back. "You married?"

"Oh yeah, 12 of the best years of my life," I answered.

"When you get home tonight, kiss your wife for me and tell her she's a lucky woman." It was more of an instruction than a comment.

"OK, I'll kiss her twice, once for you and once for me," I laughed, "Excuse me while I go get of some of this coffee."

"Don't forget," he said.

When I returned, he was gone. The waitress said he'd paid the bill for both of us. I rushed outside only to see his taillights fade into the night. All I could do was saddle up and head for home. A few hours later my bike was parked securely in the garage and I was sliding into bed next to my slumbering wife.

"When did you get home?" she asked.

"About 20 minutes ago," I said kissing her gently," Go back to sleep. By the way, I'm supposed to tell you you're a lucky woman and this is from a stranger," as I kissed her again.

"What are you talking about?" Now she was a bit more alert, so I told her his story.

"So what's his name?" She asked when I'd finished. "Where's he from ? Maybe we should have him over for dinner sometime.

I thought about it. I never got his name, where he lives, or what he did for a living. I had no way to contact him or even begin to find out who he was.

Who knows, maybe he was you.

# THE SHORTEST ROUTE TO MADISON, WI ( via Canada )

The group assembled at the Cracker Barrel restaurant at 96th street & I-69 to plan it's strategy. Naturally, breakfast was the first priority and by 9:00 AM it was time to mount up. The group consisted of 4 Gold Wings ( 2 pulling trailers ) and 1 PC800. The riders were pumped and ready. Let the adventure begin.

North on I-69 was the first leg to be ridden and 3 hours later a break was called by the leader. How convenient there was a Honda dealer 500 yards from the I -69 exit!!! After 30-40 minutes of tire-kicking, drooling over the selection of new/used bikes, and T-shirt buying we were northward bound once more.

An hour or so later, the aroma of tenderloins lured us into Schuylers Restaurant in Marshall, MI. Not only a great lunch, but the waitress supplied us with lemonade by the gallon ( maybe the fact it was 90 degrees outside had something to do with it ). A couple of group photos and we were on the road again.

Once we left the Lansing area, we rode north on MI 27. No twists, no turns, no curves for the next 200 miles ! It was as if God was playing a cruel joke on us. At one point we stopped at a rest area to stretch our legs ( and souls ) and of course, get rid of some lunch. When we consulted the highway map we found we still had 94 miles to go instead of the 15 or 20 we had figured ! Oh well, there's a pool and hot tub waiting for us at the motel. We can do this.

As the signs told us Grayling. MI was getting ever closer, our spirits lifted. We could almost feel the cool pool water and the air conditioning in the restaurant. As we missed the exit to the motel and did a 'U' to get back to it, I had a feeling of dread. Something just wasn't right. We pulled into the lot for the Super 8 Motel and checked in. No pool ! Okay, we can handle this. We asked the desk clerk about the restaurant across the way and were told their chicken was the best around. After unpacking, all 7 of us wandered over to the truck stop/convenience store/restaurant only to be told the restaurant was under construction and would be open ' in a few months '. Okay, fine! Pre-made sandwiches, chips, cokes and a candy bar for dessert would be our reward for a long hot day in the saddle.

After a good night sleep, our merry band struck north again. A good clear morning in northern Michigan is hard to beat, I learned. Good roads, cooler weather. This is what I had imagined this trip to be.

As we neared Mackinaw City, the talk on the CB centered around the Mackinac Bridge. Five miles long, 250 feet high with steel grating in the center lanes, a most impressive structure. We spotted the top of the bridge a mile before getting to it. Once you're on it - you're committed. There's no turning back. As we crossed over it, we could see huge barges beneath us. We could even watch seagulls soaring below us. A truly odd feeling.

Once we crossed into upper Michigan, it was time for breakfast. A buffet was located in short order and with Lake Huron in view we sat down to a feast. During this time it was agreed that since we were only 50 miles away, we should make this an international trip by crossing over into Canada. Once the last cup of coffee was downed, we were Canada bound.

One hour and another bridge later, we were foreigners. A quick ride around town and some gifts at the duty free shop and we were going through customs. When asked how long I had been in Canada I looked at my watch and said ' about 40-45 minutes ', to which the customs agent replied ' didn't give you much time to spend money, eh? ' " Eh this, eh that'. Poor people can't even finish a sentence properly, eh?

Since we were this for north, we cut west on MI 28 through the center of the UP rather than backtrack to the south. A rather empty, desolate area. I could only think of two things, first, not breaking down, secondly, what this area looks like in January.

We turned south on MI 77 and then west on MI 2 to follow the Lake Michigan shoreline. As barren as 28 had been, 2 was absolutely gorgeous !

Miles of good roads, gentle curves, and shoreline off to the left 80 % of the time.  We did pull over into one of many roadside beaches to snap photos and stretch our legs.

Early evening found us checking into the Super 8 Motel in Escanaba. MI.  Finally , a pool!  And a hot tub!  Did our weary bones rejoice at this news.  After settling into our various rooms, some of us hit the pool and found that there was still a little boy or girl in us.  After the horseplay in the pool, the hot tub soaked away the days aches and pains (after 15 minutes you could've stuck a fork in me, because I was done ).

MI 35 south lead us out of Escanaba the following morning and shortly thereafter we were in Wisconsin ( of course there was the mandatory souvenir shop stop or thimble stop as they became known ).  US 41 took over from MI 35 as our road of discovery and it lead us past Green Bay and Oshkosh. At Fond Du Lac we jumped on US 151 and took it into Madison.This area of Wisconsin is just as one pictures it.  Rolling green hills, cattle, easy curves, barns, rolls of hay.

Our group arrived in Madison, WI around 7:00 PM.  Checking into the Hampton Inn, we were greeted with enthusiasm and genuine hospitality. Madison had been chosen as the site as the site of Wing Ding '96, the national rally for the GWRRA.  12,000  bikes has descended on Madison for four days and Madison was glad to have them.  Our band was just a small contingency of this festival and for the next four days we enjoyed the sights of this organized chaos.  Bikes, bikes, and more bikes.  What a way to spend a few days.

Well, all good things came to an end and sooner than we wanted to believe, it was time to head home.  But the trip wasn't over for Angie and me. We had agreed to meet some friends in Burlington, IA the evening of July 4th (what's another 300 miles?) so we said to goodbye to our group and headed south toward Illinois.

Looping around Rockford, we took IL 2 south only to fine out it was closed after about ten miles.  Another change of plans.  A back road got us to IL 88 and once again, we were on course.  At Moline we dropped south to I-74 and changed to US 34 at Galesburg.  West on 34 and an hour later we were crossing the Mississippi River into Burlington.  We met our friends and inquired as to a good place to have dinner.  The recommendation was quick in coming and in short order we were dining at ' Big Muddy ', a fine restaurant on the banks of the Mississippi.  As you enter the building you notice a yellow tape line along the wall about two and a half feet above the floor. We were told this was the water level during the flood of 1993. If you get a chance to eat at Big Muddy, be careful. The appetizers are bigger than the entrees and very bit as good. With stuffed bellies, we managed to get back to our motel in time to watch the 4th of July fireworks out of our third floor window.

Our last day on the road was spent on I-74 headed east back through Illinois to Indiana. The Indiana State line looked like a welcome home sign after being on the road almost a week. Of course, a late lunch at the Beef House Restaurant at exit 4 was one last treat of our journey. A good sandwich, a salad and some lemonade and we were ready for the last leg home to Indianapolis.

A fine trip. 1827 miles. Good friends. No mechanical problems. No personality conflicts. Lots of memories. Would I do it again? Absolutely! But probably not in January or February.

# Spring Fever

Okay, so it's March. The weather isn't cooperative, the garage needs cleaned, the wife has a ' honey-do ' list 12 pages long, and you don't even want to think about getting your tax papers together ( you've got another month for that, right ? ) So what's a guy to do? Get ready boys, get ready! There's a lot of roads to cover this season and no better time to prepare for them. Take advantage of the next few weeks and see if anything on this list applies to you.

The next rainy Saturday afternoon that comes along (and it will ) grab a state map and yellow highlighter. Spend an hour or two marking routes that look interesting. As you ride this year note the date you rode various rides. This time next year you'll enjoy reliving those rides.

Go to an office supply store and buy a $5 weekly journal. Use this as your maintenance log. When did you last change your oil? Your plugs? Your tires ? With a log it's a lot easier to keep accurate records. You can also use it to make notations about restaurants you found and enjoyed, gas stations you didn't, bike shops you had to force yourself to leave, bars your buddies had to drag you out of, etc..

Clean your bike. Most of us have a tendency to ride as much as possible and clean as little as possible. Taking a Sunday afternoon and spending it with a bucket of soapy water, some cleaning rags, a couple of towels, and some paste wax will serve more than one purpose. First, you'll be surprised at what you find when you give a bike a good thorough cleaning. A crack in a fender? A clutch cable coming loose? Excessive corrosion on a battery terminal? Frayed wiring at the brake light? A good cleaning not only makes your bike look great, but is a good safety checklist as well. If you have to see a nail head in your rear tire, wouldn't you rather see it in your garage instead of 40 miles from the next exit? Besides, in your garage you can always ask your wife to bring you some coffee and maybe a sandwich. I wouldn't push for dessert though.

Second, spending the afternoon with your bike ( even though you're not riding ) is good for the soul. No office pressures, no wife's conversation ("You know we could have bought a new bedroom suite by now with the money you've spent on that bike"), no settling arguments for the kids. No distractions. No conflicts. Just you, your bike, maybe some Bob Seger on the radio. How can a person go wrong?

Talk about biking. I mean just to people in general. I was talking with a co-worker awhile back and another person overheard. They asked if I actually rode one of those machines. Half an hour later they were asking if I thought they could learn to ride. The image we portray as riders is so critical. Too many people have a negative impression of us simply because of bad stereotypes. Every person you talk with goes away with an impression. Show them that we really are a fun group that can use words with more than one syllable.

Do some planning now. Schedule your vacation time to match the events you want to attend. Start a savings account for rally of your choice. Put a little money away each week for a Gatlinburg run this fall. Plan to try something new. Perhaps camping or a night ride. Get your wife or girlfriend involved with your sport. That in itself will open a whole new world. I guarantee it.

Of course reading magazines and watching TV sporting events go without saying. I mean, after all, it is March. That's why magazines and TV shows were created. Isn't it? And of course riding or driving to your favorite breakfast place on Saturday or Sunday morning to swap lies with your buddies is the mainstay of any true survivalist. The moral (or possibly immoral, ) support of various members is truly something to behold. Never before have so many said so much at one time with nothing to say. Yet the warm glow of camaradie surrounds us all. All I can say is be there!It's the only way to experience it.

I just asked my wife Angie, if she had any suggestions how to get through March. Her advice was to get a Trader and do a little shopping for another bike, so..........

(This is Angie Reed. That dang fool husband of mine just left to buy a Trader. He said something about striking while the iron's hot and if I wanted this article finished, to do it myself. So I am. God, give me strength.)

# THANKS FOR THE MEMORIES

OK, so you've returned from bike week in Daytona. You're trying to explain the scenery (bikini clad and otherwise ) to your buddies and failing miserably. Sure would be easier with a set of pictures, wouldn't it?

Stop and think about it for a moment. How many times have you set at a table having coffee with the guys and someone whips out his pictures of his Colorado trip? There's no way he could do justice to that kind of ride with mere words. His photos serve two purposes. First, they're a testament to his adventure. Something tangible to share with his friends. Second, he'll always have that trip with him. When the snows flyin' and the wind's blowin', they'll provide him with an escape route to better riding days.

What do you photograph ? Whatever you want! Your bike for starters. Park your bike outside in the yard or on the driveway. Grab your camera and start shooting. Shoot from various distances, various angles. Have someone stand next to it, put your helmet on the seat, anything to give it variety. Shoot at least a roll of film. Once the pictures are developed, you'll have a good idea of how to get what you see through the viewfinder onto film. Don't worry about being a professional photographer. You're not looking for Pulitzer Prize, just good pictures. Get comfortable with your camera and use it. Of course you'll pack it for a trip, but keep it handy on any ride regardless of how short. Get out ahead of your buddies, park the bike, and get pictures of them going through a particular curve. Sure it takes a bit of extra effort to do it, but the look on their faces when you show them the pictures is worth it. Get a group shot at the beginning and the end of the ride. Take one of Joe and Sam bent over checking the battery connections. Get one of the road ahead with the full canopy of autumn leaves above it. Get one of John picking up his bike after forgetting to put down the kickstand at the gas station. Take a shot of everyone having breakfast together. Don't forget to get one of the Ducati you want. Be creative. These are memories you're making, not just pictures you're taking. (If your memory is like mine, don't forget to label your pictures. Some trips may start running together.)

What kind of camera should you use ? Get a camera that is easy to operate. A price range of $30 - $ 90 will get you a basic setup. Don't worry about interchange bayonet mount 80-200 zoom macro lens. A good camera with a built - in flash and maybe an autowind feature will do all you need it to do and still small enough to fit into your jacket pocket. Today's 35 mm cameras have evolved into very reliable pieces. After shooting a couple of rolls of film, you should be pretty comfortable with any brand you select. One style on the market is a disposable camera. Buy it, use it, develop it. No loading/unloading the film. No muss, no fuss. Not a bad way to go for some of us. Keep in mind that this is supposed to be fun. Don't be too critical of your pictures. After all, their main purpose is to "jumpstart old memories." Just think, if someone had been doing this on a regular basis years ago, we would know what we could prove that I had coal black hair at one time. As for me. if you want a current portrait of my Sunday morning coffee ritual, be sure to use a wide angle lens.

# DOIN' THE WAVE

You're rolling down the interstate on your favorite mode of transportation (your bike) and you notice another two wheeler approaching you from the opposite direction. Suddenly his/her hand goes up from the handlebar and lo-and-behold a silent greeting is extended to you. You don't recognize the rider or biker and before you can react, he is gone. What prompted this anonymous act of friendship?

A simple wave of the hand can do more to lift one's spirit then one would think. If you've been riding in the rain for a few hours and suddenly see someone else in the same predicament, a wave is an instant statement that says "Yes, I am a serious rider too." As you come out of a series of tight twisties, a wave to an oncoming rider says, "you're going to have a ball the next few miles." If you see a bunch of tour bikes, their wave is telling you that you are one part of a much bigger sum. The two-finger wave received from the bent down speed demon usually means "I'd love to chat, but I'm in a hurry."

To wave or not to wave - that is not much of a question. First and foremost, only wave when safety dictates. To take a hand off the grips at somewhere like Deals Gap is not only ridiculous, it's downright suicidal. A wave to a fellow rider is a sign of pride and fellowship. As a current ad states, "NO ONE SAYS YOU HAVE TO RIDE A MOTORCYCLE," To those of us who do, there is a certain comraderie that extends to all riders regardless of the mount they choose. This simple gesture is the acknowledgment of that bond. A wave to another rider tells him that he's not the only one that feels the call of the road or the need to ride. And don't forget children in cars with their parents. How many future riders are created by a simple act of friendship? You may never know, but wouldn't it be nice if more people thought of motorcyclists as friendly folk as opposed to " those guys on their Harleys. " (Most of the public still view us as extras from a certain Marlon Brando movie).

The next time you're out enjoying the road and notice a headlight coming towards you, take a moment and give a friendly salute to the rider. With any luck, I'll remember to wave back.

# DO'S AND DON'TS OF MOTORCYCLING

## (or Biking According to Murphy's Law )

Well, the streets are snowpacked, the wind is blowing, and the temperature is dropping down to 10 degrees. I guess I won't be taking the bike out today. Oh well, if I can't ride, I can at least read about it.

After rummaging through some back issues of various and sorted magazines, I started to notice some interesting items that I thought were worthy of mentioning. The following list of Do's and Don'ts certainly is not a complete one (if there ever could be such a thing), but simply a group of ideas that I believe all of us have thought about at one time or another.

Do check your fuel gauge before starting out on any ride.

Don't pass on a double yellow line.

Do check your tire tread at least once a month.

Don't forget to renew your club membership.

Do dress for the slide, not for the ride.

Don't put off that spring tune-up until May.

Do take a day long ride with no particular destination.

Don't push yourself beyond your personal limits regardless of what others may say or do.

Do plan on getting caught in the rain and be prepared for it.

Don't expect someone to help you if you're not willing to help them.

Do try to come to ride to breakfast on the weekend with friends.

Don't forget to close the gas cap. (Ask me about it. )

Do keep a maintenance or trip log.

Don't let the price of a quality helmet stop you from buying it. Convince your wife that you're worth it. (Lie if you have to ).

Do stop and ask for directions whether you want to or not.

Don't hit the kill switch at 65 mph.

Do stop and ask directions whether you want to or not. (It's worth repeating. )

Don't assume 4-wheelers can see you, hear you, or even care about you. In a confrontation they will always win.

Do check your tire pressure weekly.

Don't be too cocky the first time out after a winter's absence from the seat.

Do give gravel the respect it deserves.

Don't be surprised when your bike falls over if you forget to lower your kickstand.

Do remember to raise your kickstand before going into 1st gear.

Don't believe you can get 'one more season' out of those old break pads.

Do take off the sunglasses before sunset.

Don't jump right out at a green light. Wait a second to see who might be running a yellow light themselves.

Don't believe you have enough insurance coverage just because your agent says you do.

Do check your fluid levels & lights regularly.

Don't price replacement body parts before going to Deals Gap. At $80 for a mirror, you might become quite cautious.

Do subscribe to at least 1 motorcycle magazine. (Okay, maybe 6 )

Don't borrow your buddy's sleeping bag if you have a bladder problem.

Do buy him a new one if you did.

Don't buy a tee shirt at every event you attend. Buy two.

Do carry a Medical Alert card but hope never to have to use it.

Don't think your bike will clean itself. (See my wife, Angie)

Do use your turn signals regularly.

Don't exclude your wife or girlfriend from your biking activities. She may exclude you from other activities.

Do talk to new members. Make them feel a part of things.

Don't think that your clutch cable is going to last forever.

Do have your reasons prepared when you come home with a new bike.

Don't neglect your battery levels and connections or they may neglect you. (See me again.)

Feel free to alter or add to this as you wish. The main thing is to enjoy motorcycling and all the fun that goes with it.

# The 3 Season Rider

It's Saturday morning. All your chores were done last night and you've reserved tomorrow afternoon to cut the grass. It's 70 degrees and no rain is called for until the middle of next week. A slight breeze is coming out of the west and the bike's got a full tank of gas. Great day for a ride, Right?

Well, maybe. Anybody and everybody can, and often do, ride in such ideal conditions. After all the road calls the loudest to the person willing to listen doesn't it ? While I am as guilty as the next person about finding an excuse, any excuse, to ride anyplace, anytime and for any reason, some of the enjoyment of riding requires an obstacle or two to overcome.

Cold weather riding has its own unique set of challenges, Hypothermia can be a very serious business and shows no mercy to the unprepared. Keep this in mind when setting out on a late fall or early spring ride (or mid winter as the case may be). Dress in layers and pay particular attention to your hands, wrist, feet, and ankles. Wearing a stocking cap under your helmet will go a long way to keeping your head warm. A set of longjohns under your jeans and chaps and your legs are ready for the ride ahead. Don't let a forecast high of 30 degrees curtail your riding pleasure. As long as the roads are dry and your spirits are high, you'll have a great time. I particularly enjoy waving at 4 wheelers who can't believe their eyes as I ride past them.

Riding in the rain can be a really enjoyable time if you go into with right attitude. Pick a warm, easy, rain (avoid thunderstorms with lightning at all costs). Suit up in the garage, open the door, and head out. Get on some well paved back roads and you'll have very little traffic to deal with. Now sit back and enjoy life. Listen to the rain on your helmet as you would listen to a symphony. Different tempos at different speeds. A light opening movement followed by a strong central theme. Rain can be more than water falling from the sky if you listen to it with different ear. Once you learn this trick, riding in the rain will take on a whole new meaning.

When the thermometer starts hitting 95 degrees or higher, a different strategy is called for. Long sleeve shirts (to protect arms from sunburn), cool ties, plenty of stops, and some drinking water or Gatorade are in order for this ride. Skip that cold beer until you get home. Alcohol and riding don't mix at any time, but especially during hot weather it can be a lethal combination. Avoid cola products as well. They don't replace the fluids you need as quickly as a sports drink product. Pay attention to the signals your body is sending you. Dizzy? Can't seem to concentrate? Getting nauseous? Heat stroke could be just around the corner. Time to pull over and sit in the shade for 20 - 30 minutes. Good time to have one of those bottles of water you brought with you. Don't try to be a hero and push on. One sign of heat stroke is the inability to make a decision. To try to continue on with no break is definitely the wrong one.

Snow? Easy call. Have some more coffee and read a magazine or two. You're not going anywhere today.

As they say, any ride is better than no ride. When fate co-operates and give you superb riding conditions you certainly should take advantage of them if at all possible. But when you reflect on your previous rides, the most memorable ones usually involve some form of inclement weather. As you listen to other riders, the most intriguing stories often start with "Back in February, it was 28 degrees when we started out for Bike Week," or "Last August, it was so hot I would have sworn my tires were going to melt right off the bike." Don't let Mother Nature rob you of memories in the making when she throws you a curve in the weather forecast. With a little preparation, the right attitude, and some good old common sense you'll be amazed at the stories you'll have to tell. If you doubt that, ask me about riding in 33 degree below zero wind chill factor without any electrics. Talk about a story.

# The Unpardonable Sin

It's Tuesday night. I know that tonight I'll be able to sleep. My penance is served. The nightmare is over. My wife owns a bike. Again. Allow me to explain.

The love of my life, the flame of my fire, the object of my desire, (she types these stories, you know) my wife, Angela, took the ABATE motorcycle education course July of last year. She had the usual fears and apprehension, but with my constant encouragement and skillful tutoring (hope she keeps that line in here) she passed the course with flying colors. Or, maybe in spite of them. Regardless, we had a deal. The day she graduated the course, I would have a bike in the garage for her, and not my Goldwing either. Something of her very own.

Well, a deal's a deal. When she come home Friday night with her certificate in hand, there was a 1983 Honda CM250 waiting for her. Purple and silver, belt drive, mini faring, trunk, engine guards, highway pegs, am fm cassette, throttle lock, more chrome than you can imagine, and only 7500 miles. She was in love (and she even liked me, once again).

Saturday morning wouldn't come fast enough, but it finally arrived. Her first ride with her husband and 2 "big brothers" ( Bill Lane and Tom Wager ) was at hand. We backed the bike down the drive, she swung her leg over, checked the kill switch, turned the key on, hit the starter button, and nothing. Not a crank, not a groan, not a click, not a whine, other than from me. The battery was shot. I never knew disappointment could be so quiet and so loud at the same time. Angie turned and looked at me as if to say "Well, what are YOU going to do about this? We are going to ride today, RIGHT? "But she never said a word. She didn't have to. I knew that some way, somehow I would get a battery in that bike, and I would do it fast. Sure enough, Tom and I located and installed a new battery in less than an hour. Angie touched the starter button and the 250 roared to life. All disappointment had vanished. An ear to ear grin beamed in it's place. We were off.

That day was 2500 miles ago. During the next few months, Angie was always riding. The more she rode, the better she got. The better she got, the more she rode. It was becoming a vicious circle. Dinners became later and later. Weekends revolved around riding. Morning conversations centered on gas mileage and after market parts. Honda spray cleaner became more prevalent then Endust. If a sweatshirt lacked the Honda Logo, it was not quite appropriate apparel. Wind chill factors took on a whole new meaning. What was once referred to as "rather unflattering" now became lovingly called "my Grumpy Old Men suit ". Yes, a monster had been born. And I would have to learn to deal with it.

O.K. I can do this. One of the more common discussions over morning coffee was lack power. "Yes, it's a great bike" Angie would say, "but I have a hard time keeping up with everybody. Maybe I need something a little bigger. Nothing fancy, just a bit bigger." Say no more. If that's not an open invitation to go bike shopping, than I never heard one before. With the gauntlet hurled in such a manner, as they would say in England, the game was afoot.

During the course of the season I had been offered a good price if I ever wanted to sell the CM250. With the thought of a newer bike in mind, I called the gentleman and the deal was done. He picked it up on a Saturday when I was out of town. Upon my return. I was informed how bare the garage now looked. Parking my Goldwing did nothing to alleviate the cloud of gloom that seemed to now hover over our home. No problem. I can replace the lost ride in short order.

At least that's what I thought at the time. My friends, if you choose to believe only one thing that I have ever or shall ever write, let it be this. NEVER, NEVER, SELL YOUR WIFE'S BIKE WITHOUT IT'S REPLACEMENT ALREADY PARKED IN YOUR GARAGE!!!! Rack up her charge cards, forget her birthday, miss your 25th anniversary dinner, display the high school picture that won her the stupidest grin honor, tell her friends her actual weight or true age, but never, I repeat, never leave her bikeless for more than 30 - 40 minutes. The withdrawal is to gruesome to describe. Small children and the weak of heart should not be allowed any form of contact for a minimum of 7 days. It takes that long for the side effects to wear off. I can testify to this because it took me 30 days to locate and purchase the correct replacement for her CM250 (in my defense, my only guideline was "you know what I want - go work your miracles". Not a lot to go on).

Yes, we drove 350 miles round trip just to look at a bike. Yes, I bought a Trader every week for a month. Yes, I had people in 3 states in the lookout. Yes, I bought a bike, put it in the garage, and took it back the next day. Yes, we looked at every bike shop within 50 miles. Yes, I called every bike shop within 100 miles (and have the phone bill Evel Knevel couldn't jump over). Yes, I asked for divine intervention on a regular basis. And then the clouds parted and a ray of sunlight burst into my bleak and morbid existence.

Finally, a voice in the wilderness (one Joe Prindle, a top bike wrench ) told me of a '85 Honda 650 Nighthawk that was available. Low miles, oil cooled, shaft drive, great shape. A quick consultation and I felt redemption was at hand. Not only did he recommend it, but he actually owned one for several years and loved it. Not a lot of extras according to him, but that's half the fun of buying a bike. Angie can "dress it" to suit her style of riding and I can pay for it. What a deal. Seems like I'm always on this end of deals with her. That's O.K. I'm finding that I'm reliving my early riding days thru her. I often discover that her enthusiasm is contagious and brightens my rides with her. It's really nice to have a "Riding Buddy" so handy.

Hopefully, the 650 will hold her awhile. If she starts eyeing my Goldwing, I don't know what I'll do. But I can guarantee you one thing. There won't be any vacancy on her side of the garage. Did I say her side of the garage? I remember when it was my garage. I'm not quite ready to concede that point yet.

# A Midsummers Ride

It's Wednesday night.  Nothing on tv but repeats.  You mowed the grass yesterday and the wife, believe it or not, has no chores for you to perform.  You want to do something, but knowing you have to work tomorrow, you don't have a real high ambition level.

No problem!  It's summer in Indiana!  Warm temperatures and late sunsets.  Get on your favorite bike, top off the tank and try this quick getaway.  Depending on where you live, you'll still be home in time apple pie ala mode before calling it a day.

Start west on I-70 from Indy.  Go to IN267 and head south to IN42.  A pretty basic ride.  On IN42 head west again and settle into the bike.  The ride will start to pick up from this point.  Once you've passed through Monrovia, you've got a few miles of straight riding, but don't get discouraged.  The best is yet to come.

Staying on IN42, you'll go through Crown Center, Little point and Eminance.  Glance off to the right and notice the traffic on I-70.  Not a pretty sight.  Aren't you glad you're here and not there?  Feel the countryside around you and surrender to it's tranquility.  No pressures, no deadlines, no four-wheel crazies pushing you.  Just you, your bike, and good roads ahead.

Once you're past Eminance, IN42 makes a ninety degree curve to the west (this will not have been you first one).  About ten miles later you'll cross US231.  Now the real fun begins.  For the next six miles you'll be turning, braking, shifting, and pushing yourself continuously.  And loving every moment of it (there is no penalty for laughing out loud).

As you approach Cunot, slow her down a touch. You'll be turning north on IN243 here. When you overshoot your turn (and it's easy to do) don't panic. Go on another mile or so and slowly cross the bridge over Cataract Lake. Take a moment and enjoy the view. Particularly if the sun only has another hour or so of life left this day. Turn around and head back to IN243. North on this road will take you back to I-70 in about five or six miles. You'll pass Lieber State ark and ride between some towing pines. This road hold a few surprises for you,, so don't get too complacent and of course, watch out for the deer. They're not as tame as their West Virginia cousins.

At I-70, head back east to Indy (if you must) and fifty minutes later, you'll be choosing whether you want I-465 north or south. A short time later, your toughest decision should be whether or not to heat the slab of pie before applying a generous scoop of ice cream to it. With this ride under your belt, it's not that tough of a choice.

# Decisions, Decisions

Sometimes you have to make a choice. Left or right. Up or down. North or south. In or out. Right or wrong. Well, here's a choice that gives you no wrong answers.

Start out early on a Saturday morning. Leave from Indianapolis and head south on St. Rd 135. Give yourself an extra 30 to 40 minutes once you've arrived in Bargersville to have breakfast. You'll find a handy little diner on the southwest corner of St. Rd 144 and St. Rd 135 (look behind the car wash). Good food, good prices, great atmosphere. Be sure to ask for peanut butter for your pancakes. They'll understand.

After breakfast head south on 135 again and get ready for Nashville. Hopefully you won't be detained by all the shops. Remember, this is a bike trip not a shopping trip. On the south end of town you'll turn left onto St. Rd 46. Go about 3 &1/2 miles and gas up at the Shell station on your left. You're going to need it. Another 1/2 mile and you'll turn right, putting you onto St. Rd. 135 again. Now settle back and enjoy 24 miles of some of the finest sport touring roads Indiana has to offer. You'll eventually come to St. Rd. 58 and you'll want to turn right for the next leg of the journey.

Surprise!! 135 was just a warm up for St. Rd. 58. You've got 16 miles of twisties, turnys, ins, outs, ups, and downs ahead of you. By now you'll have been on the road a few hours so the sun should be pretty much overhead ( you wouldn't want to do this looking into a setting sun, trust me.). You may even want to stop in Zelma and grab a cold drink and take a break. Might check the tread on you tires just to be sure you're taking the curves on the inside (ask Tom Wager about his theory of mileage vs. curves ). O.k. breaks over. Time to saddle up again. Just a few miles and you come to St. Rd. 446. Take a right here and sit back for a bit. Your steering head bearings won't be getting such a workout for awhile St. Rd. 446 will stretch out for 20 miles of easy, laid back, reflective riding. Going over Monroe Reservoir, you just can't help but grin and feel God spent a few extra minutes on this area. He may have had motorcyclists in mind as He laid out this part of the state. You'll find you come up to St. Rd.46 a little quicker than you want to. Hang a left here and follow it back thru Bloomington to St. Rd. 37. North on 37 and 40 minutes later you'll be ordering chicken and noodles with fresh rolls ( not biscuits ) at the Bob Evens restaurant at 31 & 465 on the south side of Indianapolis ( or at least I would be ).

# OR

You've finished your breakfast in Bargersville and realize you really don't have a much time as you thought (that honey do list does start to wear on your conscience after awhile). No problem, head south on 135 as planned. Go threw Morgantown and take a right on st. rd. 45 in Bean Blossom. Follow this great road for a bit and you'll be tempted to neglect those "Honey do's" for just a longer. Not to worry. You'll still be back in plenty of time to knock a few of them out. And you'll be grinning as you do them. Back to the road. Watch out for those train tracks. They're not bad, but you make a hard left just past them. Continue on and don't be impatient, there's a little something up ahead waiting for you. Once you get to Bloomington, you'll want to turn right on Walnut St. (look for an Ace Car Rental on the corner ). Take Walnut to the stoplight for old scenic highway 37 ( if you get to dual lane 37, you've gone 1 mile to far - turn around and go back, it's worth it ) turn right and prepare your self for 17 miles of hidden curves, twisted corners, goats in the road ( yes, I said goats ), and a few items that I'll just let you discover on your own. I will tell you the road is well paved and gravel from the local driveways is at a minimum. The road eventually spills out on St. Rd. 37. A right turn here gets you to that chicken and noodles in about 30 minutes.

As I said earlier, sometimes you have to make a choice. With these 2 rides there is no wrong choice. Just a long one or a short one. Both are equally enjoyable and yet have their own "feel" about them. Now I have to make a choice. Where to take Angie for dinner. I don't know. That chicken and noodles is sounding pretty good.

# An Annual Odyssey

It's 5:00 Saturday October 19th, 1996. I'm thinking about all my H.S.T.A. friends warming themselves around the bonfire at Margy's cookout. Me? I'm standing in 2 inches of snow on the edge of Cheat Mountain in West Virginia staring at my Goldwing lying on it's side. As the wind picks up and the snow starts coming down faster, I find little consolation that in a few more minutes it will be to dark to see it. The temperature is falling faster than a skydiver with no parachute and my buddy and I are 50 miles from anywhere that is even remotely civilized. "Are we having a good time yet?" I ask Jay. He growls an appropriate response.

But I'm ahead of myself. What say we start at the beginning.

My good friend and stalwart companion, Jay Powell, and I have a tradition that we've managed to maintain over the past few years. Once a year we take a trip together. No wives, no other friends, no children, no distraction. Usually this trip will last 3 or 4 days. This adventure is our time to recharge our souls and spirits and year after year it never fails to accomplish that task. This year, the Blue Ridge Parkway was to be out destination.

We pulled out of Indianapolis Friday morning about 9:30 a.m. (of course we were supposed to leave at 8:30 but a minor repair to a mirror delayed our departure). We would only have 3 days to get to the Blue Ridge and back so interstate travel was called for. 74 east to 275 south around Cincinnati to 75 and south on 75 from there. Just a few miles into Kentucky I could hear my stomach rumble, so a lunch stop at Thad's restaurant was in order (great clam chowder on the salad bar, at least that was my opinion after the 3rd bowl). Plenty of coffee and good prices. A good 1st stop. With the temperature never getting above 45 degrees we know we would be making a few more before the day was out.

75 south lead us to Lexington where we jumped onto 64 and headed east. Good roads here and great scenery. Rolling hills with autumns best colors out in abundance. About 60 miles east of Lexington it was time for gas, coffee, and a toe inventory. I hadn't felt mine since Lexington. The shell station at Morehead, Kentucky was an easy choice for gas, but what about coffee? No problem. 100 yards south of the shell station was a place called "Cutters Roadhouse". Well, we both had our chaps on anyway, so why not? We walked in and knew immediately we'd found the right place. Peanuts on the tables, shells on the floors (You know you're in a Roadhouse when the men's room door says "BUBBA'S"). As we ordered our coffee the waitress asked if we were cold "riding them motorcycles out there"? We would get that question every place we stopped for the next 3 days. Once we warmed up and felt more humane towards the world we asked for our checks. The manager came over and told us the coffee was on the house and anytime we were in the area to stop in, there would always be hot coffee waiting for us. We thank her profusely, tipped the waitress generously, and saddled up once again.

For the next 200 miles it would be ride an hour, warm up 20 minutes, ride some more, warm up some more. Eastern Kentucky and West Virginia have some of the prettiest countryside one could ask for, I can imagine what the state roads must be like. Eventually we came to Charleston, West Virginia. A Bob Evans Restaurant served as the dinner stop. Another 80 miles and we were in Lewisburg, West Virginia with a Day Inn being the evening's destination.

Saturday morning broke with crystal clear blue skies and a promise of 60 degrees by the afternoon We were elated. Just 100 miles to ride and we'd be on the Blue Ridge Parkway. We even had energy to clean our bikes!! It was going to be a glorious day.

Breakfast was hurried to say the least. We could eat that anyplace, anytime. Taking 60 east out of Lewisburg we ended up at Buena Vista, Virginia. Another 5 miles out of town and we were there. Stopping for the mandatory pictures at the entrance we learned a quick lesson.. Always have your partner watch your back if you're standing in the road to take a picture. Some four wheelers don't understand the need for those "tourist " type pictures. Back in the saddle and away we went.

As we began our ride we both couldn't stop grinning. The weather was ideal, the colors were spectacular, the views breathtaking. The parkway was in perfect condition. Some twists and turns, but nothing to difficult. Traffic was surprisingly light much to our enjoyment. Some areas engulfed you in a tunnel of leaves while others gave you views that seemed to go on forever. A little Jim Brickman in the tape deck ( Bob Seger would have been a bit strong ) and one could truly "get lost in it all". I know I did.

About 10 miles from the north end of the parkway, we pulled into a vitistors center to kick back and discuss what we had seen. A small boy pointed at my Goldwing and said "motorcycle, motorcycle". With his parents consent, I put him on it and watched him grin from ear to ear. A few moments later his parents thanked me for my kindness and taking their son with them headed towards their car. I overheard the wife say "That certainly was nice of that man" to which her husband replied " Yeah, I guess some of them are O.K. people". It never hurts to show a stranger the friendly side of riding.

As Jay and I walked over to the map of the Parkway, we had the surprise (or so we thought) of the ride. We had entered the Parkway at mid point !! There was an entire south end we hadn't ridden!! And now time was running out if we were to get home by Sunday night as planned. Oh well, that will give us a reason to come back next year.

Once we left the parkway we had a decision to make. Back to the interstate or take 250 across the mountains. Since we had been on interstate constantly and neither of us had been on 250 before, we plotted to take that route. Real smart. 4000 foot elevation cold temperatures, rain off and on, and only 4 hours of daylight left. Yeah, real smart.

We first noticed the snow about 2 hours after leaving the Blue Ridge. It was like the sunlight stopped at the West Virginia state line. O.K, What's a small flurry here and there? We've been in tougher situations. Besides, Elkins is only 50 miles away and I know we'll be able to find a motel there. Just a little further. Just a little higher. That flurry is now snowfall. Maybe we should turn around. Naw, Elkins is only 35 miles away now. We pull out of the rest area (around here we'd call it a wide spot in the road) and press on. Once we get over Cheat Mountain, it will be all downhill from there. Literally. Something about that name though. Cheat Mountain. Who would name a mountain "Cheat"? As we make our way up the edge, the snow turns serious. The road freezes and even in 1st gear, you can't keep any traction. A moment later, Jay, who is in the lead, disappears around a curve. I apply a touch of throttle and the next thing I know, I'm watching my Goldwing slide on it's side towards the edge of the mountain (unknown to me, Jay is going thou the same thing 200 yards ahead of me). After the eternity it took to slide 10 feet in slow motion, I realize that my bike is not going to go over the side of the mountain. A few deep breaths and we're where this story began.

Picking the Goldwing up (adrenalin is really good stuff) and standing it upright I was amazed at the lack of damage. A loose highway board and a scrape on the lower left cowling. That's it. No big deal. Jay's '83 GL1100 suffered a scrape on the upper left fairing. These Goldwing are very forgiving bikes. With some help from a local four-wheel we got both bikes turned around so they were facing down the mountain. For the next 1&1/2 miles we straddled our bikes and coasted down the 3 foot gravel edge to get below the snow line. Once there, we could ride the wet road to a motel. Of course that turned out to be 60 miles away!! Cold, wet, tired, hungry, and a bit confused we had no choice but to keep going. Jay stopped at a church that was having services and recruited a couple to lead us to Marlington, West Virginia where I had finally made reservations. Once we pulled into the motel parking lot, we found that our hands were to numb to shake hands with Dot and Guy Ervine, the fine folks who guided us there. I'm sure no one would recognize our signatures on the motel registration forms. The clerk informed us that the restaurant had just closed, but they'd be glad to fix us something if we wished. We wished, believe me. After shucking wet chaps, wet gloves, and wet coats in our room's, we went into the dining room to be seated in front of a 5 foot fireplace. I propped my wet boots on the hearth and watched the steam come off of them. As we thawed out with some hot coffee and good food we could finally relax and talk about the days events. Glad to be alive has 2 distinct and separate meanings, I learned. This morning was to appreciate all the wonders of nature that surround us and this evening, life itself. More than a little time was spent in front of the fire, I can tell you.

Jay and I both slept the sleep of exhaustion that night and awoke to a rainbow above the motel the following morning. Off in the distance we could also see the snow on the mountaintop. It looked a lot prettier from this vantage point.

Heading south on 219 out of Marlington Lewisburg was only 60 miles away. But, this 60 miles of 20 - 30 MPH on mountain roads. By the time we got to Lewisburg we both had had enough of the mountains. All we wanted was to get on 64 and crank up the throttle. Once on 64 that's what we did.

The weather was still cold and wet, but now we were men on a mission. Gas and coffee. Gas and coffee. Of course, we did stop to eat at Cutter's Roadhouse in Morehead Kentucky. Jay strongly recommends the ribs and the Sante Fe chicken I had was truly enjoyable. And yes, they remembered us. The coffee was free and our cups were never empty.

That Sunday, we covered 540 miles in about 11 hours. Not a real feat in good weather, but admirable (if not foolish) when you consider the inclement weather and wind chill factor. As always, it was good to get home. This trip, however, will always hold a special memory for me. With everything Jay and I enjoyed and endured it reminded me of the value of true friendship.

THANKS J. P.

# A Christmas List

My wife keeps telling me I'm hard to by for. I would disagree. I may be picky or exacting but certainly not difficult. I never (well, almost never) have a problem buying myself just the right item. I know what I want or what I need and I buy it. No problem. She, on the other hand, usually ends up taking the item back and exchanging it for a different size or color or style, or, even worse, she makes me take it back. Well, maybe the following list can take some of the confusion and worry out of your (and her) holiday shopping.

Magazine subscriptions. Pick out 2 or 3 magazines you enjoy and lay them out in a conspicuous place, say on your wife's favorite chair. When she picks them up to sit down, slide in a casual "Great, you've found them, I've been looking for those all week. I really should get a subscription to these instead of buying them off the rack. Be a lot cheaper, you know."

Good riding gloves. Keep in mind you'll need a light weight summer pair and a heaver winter set. There's 2 separate gifts right there (4 if wrapped cleverly).

A good bike cover. A cover is a novel gift because it says "O.K., you're done riding for the season right?" as she's handing it to you. With any luck your reply will be "Heh, now I can cover my bike at those motels on the road". Same gift - different interpretations.

A spare key to your bike. I've never had to use mine, but it's nice to know it's there should I need to. Besides, it's cheap insurance against losing your original key. Always better to have and not need than to need and not have.

A good spray cleaner. Simple. Effective. Always needed

A locking bike cable. I would recommend at least a 10 foot length. That way you can lock 2 bikes together or lock your bike to a post or tree. Be sure it has some form of coating so that the finish on your bike is in no danger.

Face shields. Be sure the gift giver knows the difference between a 3/4 helmet and a full face helmet. If you wear a full face, be sure they have the brand and model number. Most of us go through 2-3 shields a season and it's so nice to have a new one at your fingertips when you need it.

A current road atlas. More than once I've referred to mine on even a short trip. Besides, once you've pulled it out to check the mileage or the route, someone is bound to offer to read it for you since they can't bear to see your face all puckered up as you squint to read all those little teeny tiny numbers.

A daily journal. You'd be surprised at the information you'll put into one. Maintenance records, mileages ran, restaurants you enjoyed, weather conditions. people you met on the road, etc. Reading it the following year is like reliving your various rides. You'll be amazed at the memories that will rise back to the surface.

A gift certificate for a good bike cleaning. Over the years my wife has given me handmade certificates for car washes, a favorite meal, yard mowing, a weekend out ( one of my favorites) with the guys, a special evening ( don't ask ), get out of an argument free card, breakfast in bed, and my favorite, the " YOU WERE RIGHT " card. Just be sure there's no expiration date. I tried to cash a "free back rub certificate" once and got laughed at because it had expired.

A set of tires. A lot of dealers run tire specials during December, January, and February. You can purchase a set and they will store them until you need them. It's nice to know you've got a set waiting for you anytime you need them. Of course, be careful if you're thinking about trading bikes. Most dealers will be glad to accommodate the change in size or style, but confirm this option BEFORE the purchase is made. A new battery would fall into this category as well.

A camera. Nothing to elaborate. Maybe a basic 35 mm. without to many bells and whistles. Something small enough to fit into a shirt or jacket pocket. Self winding and auto focusing would be nice. A built in flash would be handy, too.

A flashlight (yes Angie, I know I've got 10 or more). A mini mag style is a good choice. Sturdy and easy to operate. Small enough to tuck on your bike or in your gear without taking up a lot of room. It's the kind of item you don't need until you need it. And then you really need it.

A good quality tire gauge. Not one of the stick things, but something accurate and dependable. Of course, you have to remember to use it (something I'm still trying to do).

Car wash coupons. It really doesn't have a lot to do with bikes, but there's something about driving a clean car or truck that brightens ones' outlook on life. Pull in, let the machine do the work, hand the cashier a coupon. It doesn't get much easier than that.

An electronic Rolodex ( I can't believe I'm recommending this ). Punch in various names, phone numbers, address, dates, etc. Once stored in this manner, you'll always have that information at your fingertips. They're small and compact enough to carry with you anywhere. Even I have to admit I have one for business use and am quite pleased with it.

A map of the United States. Something big enough to read easily but not so big you can't hang it on your garage wall. As you make various trips through out the country, route them out with stickpins or color dots on the map. After a few runs, you'll have quite a conversation piece. Plus, every time you walk by it, you'll have a flashback of the various adventures you've been on.

The list could go on and on, but you've got the idea by now. Traditional gifts are fine, but special and unique gifts are what Christmas memories are made of. The next time your spouse or current significant other complains that they have no idea what to get you this year, show them this list. If they still can't come up with something, tell them to call me. I'll tell them what I want. I've even marked some catalogs to prove it.

And of course MERRY CHRISTMAS TO ALL !!!!!!!!

# The Getaway

If you're like me, work keeps getting in the way of your riding time. Granted, motorcycling isn't exactly a free past time. You can't just roll up to the gas pump, top off, and head out without a fair amount of currency exchanging hands and that currency has to come from somewhere. The expression "ride to live and live to ride" could easily be changed to "ride to work and work to ride". For most of us, this means working 40 or more hours a week. Doesn't leave much time to ride, does it?

Well, if you are short on quantity, make up for it with quality. The best way to do this is to get away. I mean leave town. Get outta Dodge. It might sound a bit drastic, but before you chalk the idea off, read on. You may be amazed at how simple it can be.

Pick a weekend that the weather looks co-operative and pack a change of clothes, a travel kit, and maybe a few other things on your bike. You and your S. O. (significant other) mount up and head out. Try to be on the road by 7:00 am, so you don't miss any of that great morning riding. Your destination? Anywhere, but here. Just head north, south east, or west. It really doesn't matter. What does matter is that you carve out some time for yourself or selves. Avoid the interstates and try to use only use state and secondary roads. You've got all weekend. Why rush?

As you're riding, look around you. See that field off to the right? I wonder how many deer slept there last night? That groundhog on the left is just finishing his breakfast, but it looks like the heron standing in the creek is still looking for his. Check out the hawk perched on that telephone pole off to the left. Be careful of those squirrels playing tag along the edge of the road up ahead. Feel free to take a break next to that historical marker and stretch your legs. You won't find these things on the interstates, so now's the time to enjoy them.

Sometime around 11:00 or so, you'll be ready for lunch. This can be an adventure in itself. Pull in at a friendly looking local diner. Have a seat in a booth and order the special. I can't tell you what it will be, but I'll bet it'll taste great. One note. Pass on dessert. I know that's asking a lot, but that's coming up later. I promise.

Back on the road again. For the next few hours, just sit back and enjoy the rhythm of the road. Let it's music warm your heart and fill your soul. Other people are cutting grass, grocery shopping, painting house trims, cleaning gutters, and doing all sorts of other chores. You, on the other hand, find yourself grinning from ear to ear as you wave to the children playing in front yards of the homes you pass. Which scenario sounds like more fun to you?

Start looking for a "Mom & Pop" motel well before 5:00. There's nothing wrong with a national chain motel, but why pay for a bar or restaurant or pool if you're not going to use them. Quite often, a nice clean, comfortable local motel will cost you two thirds or less of a national brand. If you're in doubt about the quality of the accommodations, ask to see your room before you register. If the innkeeper is unwilling to let you do so, move on. There are plenty of others that will.

Once you've unpacked your bike and settled into your room, kick back and relax. Take your boots off and sit a spell. You're in no hurry. Grab a shower. Watch some TV. Catch up on the book you've been trying to read. It's up to you. Maybe your bike needs a wipe down from the day's journey. If so, ask the desk clerk if housekeeping might have a couple of spare towels or rags that you could use. More often than not, this simple courtesy will yield you all the cleaning rags you need and go along way in keeping the motel "biker friendly".

OK, so you've relaxed all you can and now it's time to reward yourself. Grab the phone and ask the desk clerk to recommend a good restaurant for dinner. Maybe one that is known for it's house specialties. You can bet that they've heard that question more then once and can point you in the right direction.

After you've finished that steak, slab of ribs, pot roast, orange roughy, or fried chicken (depending on the part of the country you're in), it's time for that dessert I promised. Apple pie, coconut cream pie, pecan pie, peach cobbler, cherry cheesecake, any of these will compliment that last cup of coffee ever so nicely. Ala mode' did you say? Absolutely.

Back in your room, it's time to reflect. You've had a great day. You've been on some good roads and never once did a ringing phone distract you. Granted, no chores got done, but the best memories are not made pushing a lawnmower. You got to spend some quality time with your special someone and enjoy each other's company on an entirely different level. You may have only covered a few hundred miles, but you ended up a world away. As Jimmy Buffett would say, "changes in latitudes, changes in attitudes". Think about it. Replay the last ten hours in your head and ask yourself, can it get any better than this?

Yes! You get to do it again tomorrow on the way home. Yahoo!!

# Reflections {or Stages}

The longest journey begins with a single step. We've all heard that before. But think about it for a moment. Every journey begins with that single step. Long ones or short ones. Fun packed adventures or miserable, mind numbing miles. The common factor is that first step. That commitment. The willingness to begin a task with no guarantee of it's outcome.

Motorcycling is like that. A journey that, with any luck, can last a lifetime. You start with the unbridled enthusiasm of youth and go through various stages before the journey comes to an end. Remember feeling immortal? We were young (were? that hurts) and knew that nothing would happen to us. Why bother with a helmet or proper riding instruction? Safety gear? Not for us. Accidents always happened to someone else. Right? Then came that first taste of mortality. Fortunately we weren't hurt to seriously. Mostly scrapes, a few cuts, and some sore ribs. The bruises would heal, but the ego would remain a bit more fragile then before.

Distance riding began to replace fast riding. Of course, this envelope had to be pushed just as others in the past had been. A thousand miles in 24 hours? Sure, why not? The four corners of the country in 21 days? Ok, bring it on. Somewhere along the road, we realized that covering a great distance in a short amount of time might get you some bragging rights and wear out some expensive tires, but the thrill faded quickly and we were left with bikes that had lots of numbers on the odometer and little else.

Solo riding seemed to be the thing to do next. Some of the people we rode with didn't want to see the places we had in mind or just didn't have the time available to go there, so off we went, alone. Maybe it was a bit scary at first, but we soon came to enjoy the solitude. The feeling of just picking up and going at a moments notice, stopping when ever we felt like it, staying as long or as short as we wanted to, riding as far or as little as we saw fit, that was the life. Yes, it was good to be the "lone wolf" out on the road. But, we eventually grew tired of the solitude and the song of the open road became a forlorn and somber piece of music. We were gathering memories on every ride, but when we looked around, there was no one with whom we could share them.

Local rides, charity rides, and group rides came our way and we learned to enjoy the camaraderie of other riders with similar interests. Odd how so many of them had traveled the same roads we had. Almost as if our journeys had paralleled each others. Talking about old bikes, various experiences, favorite roads, and so much more made us feel like we were part of something much bigger then ourselves. Not quite so alone. We had tried to describe sunsets in New Mexico, warm summer rains in Alabama, autumn in Vermont, or getting caught in an unsuspected snowfall in West Virginia to other non riders, but to no avail. They had no clue about the wonder of "being there", and now we were surrounded by people that needed no explanation. They had not only "been there", but were anxious to return.

"So many roads, so little time". That phrase rings true with so many of us. So many places you haven't seen. So many adventures yet to experience. So much to see and do and so little time. And finally, you get it. That elusive answer to the question you've been asking yourself these many years. You finally come to realize that each ride is the best ride you've ever been on. The saying" "there are no bad rides, just some better then others" takes on a special meaning to you. When you hear a guy whine about being cold and wet, you smile quietly to yourself. That guy over there telling about his 800 mile ride, the kid with the gauze on his forearm, the couple in their matching vests, all give you an inner peace. You know that they are part of you and you are a part of them. All of you are taking the same ride regardless of where you're at on the journey. You say to yourself, what an incredible and wondrous adventure I've been on. It's been more fun than I could have possibly imagined all those years ago. Now, I can't wait to see what's coming up around the next bend in the road.

Guess what? Me, too.

# Cold Hands, Warm Heart

OK, it's 9:00 on Sunday night. My wife, Ang, had prepared a fine dinner consisting of salad, green beans, au gratin potatoes, and grilled chicken breasts. Being the dutiful husband that I am [or try to give the illusion of], I went above and beyond the call of duty in my efforts to empty all the contents of each of the bowls placed on the table. But, alas, I am a mere mortal and had to admit defeat before dessert could be served.

What does this culinary indulgence have to do with motorcycles you ask? Considering that only 8 hours ago, a warm meal was just a dream, everything. Allow me to explain.

A clearing sky with rising temperatures promised by the local weatherman is a wide-open invitation to ride in anyone's book. In fact, it's the 1st chapter in mine. With my Goldwing's gas tank topped off and a favorite destination in mind, I started the ritual of dressing for a cold weather ride. Long johns, jeans, and chaps had served me well in the past and I saw no reason to doubt that they would fail me today. A shirt and sweatshirt under my insulated Hondaline riding coat would certainly fortify me against the 40-degree temperatures I would be encountering. Stout gloves and a face shield on my helmet, and I was dressed for battle. Decked out in all my gear, I throw a leg over my Goldwing and had a vision of a 14th century knight mounting his trusty stead. Maybe it was the extra weight of my "armament" or that I knew the "degree dragon" was lurking out there waiting for me. No matter. There is something special about this ritual and regardless of how many times I do this dance; the music of the upcoming rides always excites me.

35 degrees on a spring morning doesn't sound so bad after a month of snow and ice. With the roads finally dry enough to ride; I started out towards Skyline Drive. This road is off the beaten path and is a 90-minute ride from my front door. At least, it is in 75-degree weather. In less than 20 minutes however, I realized that 90 minutes might be a bit optimistic. As in no freaking way! Within an hour, my cool spring ride thoughts were turning more towards hot coffee and a break from the overcast skies that had refused to burn off as promised then turning miles.

My break came at a local restaurant that I had patronized on numerous occasions. The spectacle I made as I removed layers of gear was quite a show, I'm sure. Oh well, it wasn't the first time I've been stared at in public and I'm sure it won't be the last [I am talking about motorcycle related staring here]. Ever notice what a great hand warmer a hot cup of coffee makes? I will certainly testify to its healing powers, both physically and mentally. After a 30-minute warm-up, it was time to saddle up again. Ok, I can do this. Once again, into the fray, my friend

Well, the radio guy says its 39 degrees with a wind chill of 18. And that's if you're standing still. Somehow, I gotta believe that riding at 60 mph dramatically lowers the wind chill, but I have no desire to know the exact numbers. Let's just say it's

a wee bit colder than I had hoped it would be when I started out this morning. But I was on a mission and had already passed the halfway point. Odd how once you're closer to there then here, one can easily justify pushing on.

Skyline Drive brought sunshine and warmth. Well, at least sunshine and no wind. This road twists and turns as it rises above Brownstown and gives you a spectacular view of the town and adjoining Brown County. I try to ride it at least once every 3 months or so just for the view itself. The changing of the seasons viewed from it's vantage point have always given me a sense of continuity, a feeling of order. Today was no different. I could see life beginning again after its winter nap. Not jostling or vibrant. More like yawning and wiping the sleep from one's eyes. As if the land were stretching it's arms, scratching it's head and saying " Glad to see you and all, but you're a bit early, aren't? Come back in a few weeks and we'll spend some quality time together." Not wanting to intrude to long, I pointed my Goldwing towards home.

Home. Warmth. I remembered them both. The sun disappeared behind leaden clouds and any illusion of warmth disappeared with it. This was to be a challenge ride. The gauntlet had been hurled and I no option to accept it. As I rode, I could feel the cold seep into my feet, my legs, my hands. Do I take the slower back roads home or do I brave the mixed chill of the interstate. Do I choose time or temperature? Time won the mental coin toss and I jumped onto the super slab. Wind chill be dammed, I was ready to be home.

I can't say how long it took to get home, but I can say that the sight of the garage door going up did more to warm the cockles of my heart (whatever they are) then anything else during the past hour and half. Putting the kickstand down was more an act of faith than actually feeling the side stand being lowered by my half frozen foot. The simple act of removing my helmet was a test of using frozen fingers in any resemblance of order. Windshield cleaning would have to wait till later.

After a hot shower and a great dinner (Thanks, Ang), I can now reflect on the day's events. The elation of the morning had been replaced with pleasant weariness. The overcast skies had been replaced by the glow of my wife's smile. The coldness of the ride had been replaced with coziness. Strange how two totally opposite sensations are so dependent on the other? Without cold weather riding, you cannot truly appreciate the pleasures and comforts of a fine meal in a warm home. Without winter, how can you appreciate spring? And, if you don't go away, how can you come home?

Philosophy is not my forte. I just love to ride motorcycles. However, could the two be related? I may have to ponder that puzzle for a while, perhaps over some carrot cake and coffee. What do you think?

# TWO FOR THE ROAD

Did you ever wonder why they make a motorcycle seat so long? Well, I can tell you there's a good reason for it. That extra section is not just designed to hold an extra bag or to have a cooler bungeed to it. It's true purpose in life is to give you the ability to share the magic of the road with someone special. Your wife, your son or daughter, your husband, your current significant other, whomever they may be. That seat can open a whole other world, if you give it the chance. But before you do, there are some things to consider.

Skill level. The dynamics of your motorcycle change dramatically when the weight of a second rider is added to the equation. You'll want to be sure your skill level is up to the challenge. Consider the differences in such simple things as completing a slow right hand turn, coming to a fast stop, abrupt swerving to avoid sudden obstacles on the road, even mounting and dismounting your bike. Everything you do, you do for two now. You are totally responsible for that person riding behind you. Make sure that your skill level is worthy of the trust they are placing in you.

Preparation. The Boy Scouts got it right with their motto "Be Prepared". Go over your bike before each ride [you do this anyway, right?]. Check the tire pressure, the oil, the lights, the chain, everything you would do anyway. The difference between a great evening ride and a miserable memory can be something as small as the head of a nail embedded in the tread of your front tire. Make sure that your passenger has a solid backrest and secure footpegs. These two items will not only increase his or her comfort, but will add greatly to their peace of mind. No one is going to have a good time if they're afraid that they're going to fall off every time you hit a bump or a dip in the road.

Preparation also includes gear. Pack an extra pair of gloves and a second jacket if room allows. Rain gear makes an excellent windbreak once the temperature starts to fall after sunset, but only if you remember to take an extra set along. You don't have to pack as if the summit of Mt.Ranier were the ultimate goal, but in my opinion, it is better to have and not need than to need and not have.

Destination. For your first few outings, keep it simple. A short ride to the local ice cream shop. On the next ride, maybe going out to dinner at that neat place you know 50 miles away would be in order. Nothing to long or to far. Just a casual ride along some easy roads that offer great views. After all, part of the fun is showing your new riding buddy some of the sights that keep bringing you back out on the road time and time again. Don't worry about time or distance the first few times out. If you're doing your part right, it won't be long before you hear the words "Can we ride a little longer? I'm not really ready to go back just yet." Magic to your ears, I guarantee it.

One thing. No stunts. No hot throttles. No daredevil maneuvers. The quickest way to lose a new co-rider is to scare them. If them get the feeling that you are not in complete control at all times, they will never be relaxed. And if they aren't relaxed, there won't be another ride. Period. There is a time and place for everything and this is the time and the place for confidence and control. Never mind that you may be the fastest guy at the track. Those kind of things will not score points here. With a new co-rider, points are scored with consideration, not RPMs.

There is one unspoken danger about two up riding. Some people find that riding on the back seat area is all the riding that they need and are quite content, even enthused, with that position. Those riders whose partners make that choice are the lucky ones. There are those of us who come to find that two up riding leads to a partner that decides if we can handle this motorcycling thing, they can too. Second bikes, doubled fuel and maintenance costs, outfitting that second bike, additional insurance premiums, more license plate fees. The list goes on, but I'm not complaining. My wife, Angie, reads this stuff, you know. Maybe I can talk her into an ice cream ride later. She might even let me ride up front.

# An Interrupted Ride

As I write this, I am sitting in the Trafalgar Family Restaurant in Trafalgar, IN, watching it rain. I took off on the Gold Wing this morning, hoping ride some back roads and betting that I could beat a storm front coming this way. Well, I lost that bet about 1/2 a mile back. Not able to locate a dry area to put on my raingear, I hustled to this warm haven. Good food, a friendly waitress, red and white-checkered tablecloth, and fresh coffee. Maybe this ride isn't a bust after all.

Even as the rain pours on the Wing, I have to smile. The bugs will be easier to clean off and I have to admit it was due for a bath. Now, I guess I've got a reason to perform that chore tonight. Besides, I'm in no hurry to leave this Swiss steak with mashed potatoes and gravy and green beans just yet. Hey, with any luck at all, it might even continue to rain long enough for me to savor a slab of that cocoanut cream pie that is whispering my name. And who knows what other desserts might be lurking in that display case over there. All homemade, too, I'd bet.

Off to one side, some good ol' boys are discussing the merits of a recent outing (deer hunting I would guess). Another table has a strong debate going about a local Italian Restaurant and the quantity of its specials. Two other guys are verbally jousting about who should pay their bill. A trio of grandmothers is passing around pictures of their latest quilt creations. A young couple is trying their best to look inconspicuous while holding hands under the table. Country music is on the radio. A '57 Chevy is sitting outside next to my Gold Wing and both are drawing comment from other patrons.

It occurs to me that this scene is pretty universal to us motorcycle riders. It could take place in the Ames, Iowa, Ogden, Utah, Camden, Maine, Troy, Georgia, or any number of small dinners across the country. The sounds of laughter, concern, hopefulness, and anticipation, all of these are the sounds of everyday life. But how many times do they go unnoticed? As a rider, I am often in the company of strangers when I stop for fuel or food. On a long trip, the background chatter of a local diner hangout can often remind me of the warmth and caring of my family and friends so many miles away. Kinda makes them seem a bit closer.

A glance outside confirms what my ears are telling me. The rain is coming down in torrents, or as an old man in the booth behind me just said, "It's a real toad floater out there". Where else could you hear a phrase like that but in a local diner? Even as I listen to the rain continuing it's own brand of music, I find myself waiting and delaying my departure. Just until the worst of it passes, I tell myself. Let the roads dry a bit, you know. But you and I both know the real reason. These moments on the road are special gifts to bestowed upon we motorcyclists. For a fleeting moment in time, we're home. We're safe, we're dry, we're warm, and we're part of something special and unique all at one time. It doesn't matter what our geographic location happens to be at that moment. All that matters are the warm fuzzies that have engulfed us. The smile on the old lady's face as she sips her tea confirms the fact that one cannot feel alone if you just take a look around you and let the life that surrounds you soak in.

One more cup of coffee and I've got to get back on the road. That's OK. I've been wet before and I'm sure that I'll be wet again some day. At least I've got a warm, dry place to suit up before heading out. But first, I raise my cup to this moment and to you, whoever and wherever you are. After all, this is really what it's all about, isn't it? Not miles or odometer readings, but moments and memories. I've certainly enjoyed my share of both today. Hopefully, you've done the same. And maybe the next time the weather interrupts your ride, you'll find a warm, safe haven and raise a cup to a fellow rider no matter how distant he or she may be. After all, we're all in this together.

# The One Eyed Monster

OK, so you caught me watching TV. I confess that I may watch a bit to much of the "boob tube" at this time of year, but before you condemn me to the nether reaches of human intellect, allow me to plead my case. If, after hearing the evidence I am about to present, you still find my guilty of "mind numbness", than I will submit to your judgment and hit the red power button on the remote.

Everyone watches some amount of television at one time or another. Maybe for the news, maybe for the weather [is there any truth to the rumor "If you watch the Weather Channel, you won't ride."?], maybe for a mental escape from the daily grind [ask me about "Farscape". A quanta blade would look so cool on my Gold Wing], maybe for sporting events. The question is, do you control it or does it control you? Can you have an intelligent conversation without referring to the characters on last night's sitcom? Is dinner served at the dining room table or on a tray in front of a 60" big screen TV? Does the opening theme to "ER" cause your pulse to quicken? There are certain telltale signs to look for to determine one's level of addiction.

But, hold on a moment. With a bit of ingenuity, some good can be salvaged from all that time spent staring at the one eyed monster. Permit me to elaborate. A report on a unique restaurant can be turned into a dinner ride one night. That feature on the opening of a new state park sounds like an invitation to ride out and look it over. That commercial about a car wash might remind you of a particular bike in a particular garage that needs a good washing. The special on hypothermia may have some important tips for surviving an upcoming bike trip. Of course, the road construction tips on the nightly news always helps when planning your route for that weekend ride. "American Thunder" "Bike Week" "Speedvision". Who says there's nothing good on TV?

Nothing to watch. Wrong! Go out and rent some motorcycle classics. "Easy Rider", "Then Came Bronson", and plenty of others can be found at your local video store. Or get real creative and order videos of various rallies like Sturgis or Americade or Bikeweek. These will keep you engrossed for hours and are guaranteed to "get your motor running". Even better is to grab a camcorder and tape various meetings, rallies, rides, and general gatherings that you attend throughout the year. When bad weather hits, call your riding buddies over, throw on some coffee and maybe slice up some cake [if you feel that they're worth the extra effort], and let the good times roll. You'll be amazed at the memories and laughter you'll share.

Granted, if given the choice of watching TV or turning miles on my Gold Wing, the Wing wins hands down. But try as I might, I can't seem to convince my long suffering wife, Angela, that riding in the rain can be just as relaxing to me as watching the CBS Monday night lineup. And, even though it pains me to admit it, I can't ride all the time. Even the best laid plans of mi....hold it. That phrase is taken. Let's just say that there's a time to ride and a time not to ride and leave it at that. During those non-riding times, the sights and sounds emanating from the telly can be used to further your riding adventures, if you just use a bit of imagination.

Now, if you'll excuse me, "Titus" is coming on and I have to get my TV tray set up. I think my dinner is about to be delivered and I want to get the sound level adjusted on the big screen before it gets here.

Your Honor, the defense rests.

# ANOTHER CHRISTMAS GIFT

So, I'm to be alone on Christmas, he mused. That's fine by me. I doubt that I could look another pumpkin pie in the face. He knew that Christmas was a time for family and friends. A time when old wounds were healed and new hopes were born. He begrudged neither family or friend, but this year, it would be different. This would be the first year he actually looked forward to the lights, the sounds, the music, the greetings, and all the other things that made this time of year so special.

When his wife and daughter were killed by a drunk driver 5 years ago, he could not imagine nor dream that he would ever find joy in anything again. The idea of celebrating Christmas was something that he thought died with them. Simple pleasures of life took years to rekindle within him and something as big and grand as Christmas was just to much to bear. Sure, he had helped a stranger at a gas station one night, but that was years ago and it had been a spur of the moment kind of thing. Not a planned event. Not like tonight.

As he wheeled the big touring bike around thru town and finally out onto the open road, he laughed at himself. Here I am, a grown man acting like a kid at Christmas. Well, so what? Tonight, he thought to himself, that's just what I am. One stop to make and then it's "dash away dash away all". Now he laughed at himself out loud. "I can't believe I remembered that part of the poem," he said to no one but the bike, "but it certainly fit's the mood I'm in tonight.

Turning into the cemetery, he rolled to the usual parking spot and turned off the bike. "I'll be right back," he said as he lowered the kickstand and dismounted. The walk to the two gravesites next to each other only took a moment and he knew the way well. As he walked, he remembered how he had hated to come here, but couldn't help himself. It was as though the place called to him with a siren's song and he was powerless to fight it. But the more he came, the more bearable it had become, until finally he enjoyed his quiet visitations. Now, he actually looked forward to his "visits" and found himself scheduling them in his business ledger. After all, running a business is important, but, to him, this was far more important than business.

He stood there a moment and smiled at the headstones. A quiet peace had come to engulf him here in past and tonight was no different. This was as close as he could get to them in this life and he relished this time alone with them. He knelt down next to one of them and said "I'm really going to do it, dear. I know that I've said it before and never seemed to get around to it, but this time, I mean it. See, I've even got the bike out. How's that for proof? Seems fitting doesn't it? I mean, being Christmas and all. This was always your favorite time of year and it just seems to make sense. I know you would want me to handle it this way. You know, that "every gift given is given twice" thing you always tried the beat into my thick skull. Well, I finally figured it out a few years back and now plan to make the most of it." Glancing at his watch, he said, "Gotta run dear. I'll be back soon". Stopping as the other grave, he once again knelt, "Merry Christmas, my angel," he said. "Don't be concerned about my tears, they're just my way of watering your flowers. Have fun in Heaven and I'll be back to visit with you again real soon."

Walking back to the bike, he thought about the upcoming event. It was going to be difficult to do the least, but it had to be done. And it had to be done tonight. Christmas Eve. It would be his ultimate gift. The one that most people only dream of. The kind of gift that…he stopped in mid thought. There, up ahead, was a figure. And that figure was leaning against his bike.

"I see you made it" a voice came out of the darkness towards him.

"Made it? Made it where?" he asked

"To this side of course"

"This side of what? Hey, what did you do to my bike? The plastic is all broken, the handlebars are bent, the fairing is torn off, the front rim is bent," he was getting mad now, "look at all this damage!"

"Well, accidents will do that to these things you know"

"What accident? I was just riding it 10 minutes ago before I stopped to visit my wife and daughter," he stormed " Who are you and what did you do to my bike?"

"Let's just say I'm your guide. Come with me and I'll explain everything Hurry up now, we don't have a lot of time."

"I'm not going anywhere until you tell......" Suddenly he was in a room. A quiet room with soft lights and stainless steel tables. Looking around he saw some trays with surgical instruments in them and tables with small wheels attached to the legs. Against one wall was a series of doors to small to walk thru. And they had latches instead of knobs. Then it hit him.

"This is a morgue, isn't it?" he half heartedly asked.

"Yes," came the solemn answer.

"And I'm in here?"

"Yes," his guide quietly answered.

"Why? How? When? I don't understand. I feel fine. I'm on my way to a very important gathering. People are expecting me. I have something very important to do tonight that can't wait. I don't have time to be dead"

"Quite the contrary," the guide smiled, "all you have is time now."

"No look, you don't get it. Are you telling me that I died for no good reason? There has been some kind of mistake. I have devoted the past 5 years to this project and tonight............"

"That's what they all say. "A mistake", "More time", "One more chance". I've heard them all," the guide groaned, "There is a reason that you are here now, at this moment, at this time. You can not change nor alter that fact."

"Why now? At least answer me that!"

"There is no answer that I can provide that you would understand, so instead, I will show you that at least you didn't "die for no good reason".

"When you pulled away from the cemetery entrance tonight, you forgot to hit your turn signal. A simple mistake, but one that cost you your life. The oncoming car thought you were going straight across the intersection and when you turned in front of her, there was no chance of her avoiding the collision. She is fine, a few cuts and bruises, but you were killed instantly. Her memory has blocked out the last few seconds of her life and she will wonder exactly what happened for awhile. She will live a long life and devote most of it to nursing because of the accident. You were pronounced DOA at the hospital and a quick search of you personal effects produced your organ donor card. That one decision you made 5 years ago had immense effects on so many lives tonight. Because of your gifts, a 3 year old boy will see his mother for the first time, a 4 year old girl will see her father for the first time, a 16 year old boy will use your heart and grow to be a heart surgeon one day himself, a 19 year old girl will beat her bone cancer using your bone marrow and grow to have children and grandchildren, not one, but two, people will finally get off kidney dialysis and live normal lives, one of whom will go into medical research. A 56 year old grandmother will use 1 of your lungs to help blow out the candles on her granddaughter's 16th birthday cake while your other lung will save the life of a 38 year old burn victim. Your liver will filter the blood of a recovered alcoholic turned minister who will touch the hearts of tens of thousands. Died for no good reason? I don't think so."

The man was quiet. How could he argue? Besides, what good would it do now. Best just to accept the fact and go on. Then in the distance, he heard it. Turning around, he saw it just like he'd always heard. The light. A brilliant white light that seemed to fill his very soul. And the sound seemed to be coming from within the light. He glanced over at the guide, who simply smiled then vanished. That sound. He could almost make out words. He strained to hear it more clearly. Almost. That voice, no two voices. Then he saw them, arms outstretched. Tears flowed freely, joyously. As his wife and daughter embraced him, he finally heard the 5 most beautiful words he had ached to hear for so many years.


"Hi Daddy"

"Welcome home, Dear"

# The Ultimate Touring Bike?

Gold Wing. The ultimate touring machine? Well, that's how Honda bills it. As for me, the definition of the ultimate touring machine is a bit more simplistic. I like to ride. I like to ride far and I like to ride often. As far as my old bones are concerned, ultimate equates to comfort. The more comfortable I am, the more often and farther I can ride. My GL1500SE fits my 6'2" frame just right. Granted, it may not be the choice of some riders that are, shall we say, inseam challenged or those of you who may be a bit overwhelmed by almost 900 lbs of motorcycle. Not a problem. The key to any "ultimate touring machine" is personal comfort and this big rig is not everyone's cup of tea.

Protection from the elements plays a key role in any type of touring bike. If you are bold enough [or foolish enough I've been told] to ride in 35 degree weather, you learn a whole new respect for the words "wind chill". With the stock windshield and massive fairing my Gold Wing sports, there is very little cold air stirring around in the cockpit. While a good aftermarket windshield can make a huge difference on any cruiser, you just don't have the protection from the wind on your legs that is afforded you by the lower half of the Gold Wings' fairing. On the other hand, you don't have those extra bugs to clean off when you riding in nicer weather either. There's always a trade off.

To ride means to be prepared for anything. The seemingly endless space offered by the saddlebags and trunk on my Gold Wing were designed for just this purpose. Now, I grant you that I may carry an unusual amount of extra gear with me but, hey, what's the point of having all that room if you don't use it? Besides, that extra jacket or pair of gloves or set of tools or thermos of coffee has been more than appreciated by a fellow rider when they were caught short. A lot of cruiser riders I know install saddlebags or tank bags as their first accessory and with good reason. You never can tell when that rain gear is going to be called into action and having the ability to carry it with you gives you a little more piece of mind. With the many styles of bags available for cruisers, finding the right set for your bike is the kind of problem you enjoy having.

Communication has can make or break a ride. The CB radio on my Wing gets out over a mile, so I am rarely out of range of my fellow riders. With the advances in radio technology today, a CB can be fitted to almost any bike, regardless of style. The ability to converse with your fellow riders is something that can enhance any ride. It's always nice to know that you aren't the only one that could use a bit of a break or that the road ahead has turned into pothole hell. And, is there anything better than hearing your buddy's voice over the radio late at night when you're maybe a wee bit lost and not real sure of the way back to the motel?

A touring bike can be a big 1800cc behemoth or it can be quiet little 250cc fun machine. It matters more that you ride and enjoy it than what you ride. If you've set up your bike for it, every ride can be a "tour" whether it is 50 miles or 2000 miles. Touring is all about what you want it to be, not what someone else thinks it should be. Granted, this column may be a bit bias, but my Gold Wing fits my riding needs and desires. Whether your bike is a Vulcan or a Shadow or a Road King or a Virago or a Concours, it makes no difference. Your touring ability is only limited by your imagination and preparation, not by style or engine displacement. As the saying goes "so many roads, so little time". Let's go find some new ones. I know I'm ready and so are you.

13597633R00083

Made in the USA
San Bernardino, CA
28 July 2014